D0313375

Dogs Can't Fly

Dogs Can't Fly

Katharine Eccles Horn

Copyright © 2013 Katharine Eccles Horn

The moral right of the author has been asserted.

Apart from any fair dealing for the purposes of research or private study,
or criticism or review, as permitted under the Copyright, Designs and Patents
Act 1988, this publication may only be reproduced, stored or transmitted, in
any form or by any means, with the prior permission in writing of the
publishers, or in the case of reprographic reproduction in accordance with
the terms of licences issued by the Copyright Licensing Agency. Enquiries
concerning reproduction outside those terms should be sent to the publishers.

Matador
9 Priory Business Park
Kibworth Beauchamp
Leicestershire LE8 0RX, UK
Tel: (+44) 116 279 2299
Fax: (+44) 116 279 2277
Email: books@troubador.co.uk
Web: www.troubador.co.uk/matador

ISBN 978 1780884 790

British Library Cataloguing in Publication Data.
A catalogue record for this book is available from the British Library.

Typeset in Aldine401 BT Roman by Troubador Publishing Ltd
Printed and bound in the UK by TJ International, Padstow, Cornwall

Matador is an imprint of Troubador Publishing Ltd

For Robert, Emily and Daisy, who put up with me… and for Wilfred, who thought he could fly!

1

Liar, Liar!

Danny never set out to be a liar, but liar was what everyone called him.

And lying had got him into heaps of trouble over the years, but never as much trouble as he was in at this moment, face down on the forest floor, hands and feet tied and a sack over his head. Even for Danny, this was a lot of trouble to be in.

He wondered, as he tried to remain conscious, whether it was lying that had got him into his present situation, and decided it was, indirectly at least.

Danny just loved to tell stories. From the moment he could speak, he had told them to anyone who would listen. He even told them to people who weren't listening.

He told a stranger on the bus that he was one of Santa's elves; he told the doctor that the Queen was his granny; confided to the postman that his parents kept a baby alligator in the bathtub and told his playgroup that he had once seen a snowman come alive and do Kung Fu on a badger. And this was all before he reached the age of three.

Children loved Danny's stories.

Grown-ups said, "How clever! What an imagination!"

When Danny started school, he told the class his dad was a lion-tamer. They looked at him, wide-eyed.

"Was your mum in the circus too?" breathed Jason Bradley.

It was too easy, really. "She was a tightrope walker…" said Danny, "… until the accident!"

That afternoon in the playground, Danny's mum found Jason on his knees, examining her ankles.

"Which one is it?" he hissed.

"Left," said Danny.

"You can't hardly tell!" pronounced Jason. "It looks just like a real one!"

Soon, Danny learned to use stories to get out of things he didn't like doing: a dog had eaten his school shoes; a passing eagle had flown off with his reading book; his homework had been lost in a boating accident…

The grown-ups began saying, "Liar!"

The children began saying, "Liar!"

Big Wayne Smith began chanting, "Liar, liar, pants on fire!"

Finally, even the teacher cottoned on. Danny should

never have said his sister Sam had cancer. He hadn't really meant to lie: he just couldn't pronounce tonsillitis. The teacher was so sorry for him that she gave him all the best jobs around the classroom. And then she found out the truth.

Danny's parents were called in to school. It was the first of many times.

"What did you say a thing like that for?" his mum asked him.

"The other word was too…"

"Too what?" stormed his dad. "Too boring for you?"

"Too hard," said Danny, but they weren't listening.

"You're not normal, you," said Danny's mum. But Danny knew that already.

No teacher ever felt sorry for Danny again. Instead they blamed him for everything. By the time he reached the end of primary school, he had had more detentions than hot dinners. Literally. The children had stopped asking him to play because they didn't trust him. Gradually Danny was pushed to the edge of things, and, when you are on the edge of things, you are easy for the bullies to spot.

Wayne Smith and his gang of assorted thugs homed in on Danny.

"Liar, liar, pants on fire! Liar, liar, Danny Squire!" It was lucky for them that Danny's surname rhymed with liar – they would never have been bright enough to come up with the rhyme otherwise.

The other children copied Wayne, because it was less painful than arguing with Wayne. Soon Danny's nickname was Pants-on-Fire and the chant of 'Liar, liar' followed him wherever he went.

And then last September, Danny had started high school and Wayne and his gang had taken his dinner money every day. If Danny didn't hand it over, they thumped him. If he did hand it over, they usually thumped him anyway. After a month of starvation, Danny persuaded his mum to give him packed lunches. The first day, Wayne stole all the good bits, then emptied the rest on the pavement and stamped on it. Next day, Danny scoffed his lunch on the way to school and Wayne punched him in the stomach until he was sick.

"Why don't you tell the teacher?" asked Jason, as he shared his crisps with Danny.

"What's the point? They don't believe a word I say."

Yes, it was definitely the lying that had started it, because the lying had caused the bullying, and the not-doing-very-well-in-school, and those things in turn had caused his dad to bring home the cardboard box. And that was where his current trouble had really started, with the cardboard box.

2

Cardboard Box

It arrived on a Friday evening. Danny's dad carried it in with a great silly grin on his face.

"I bought it off this bloke I met out on the road!"

Danny rolled his eyes. His dad, Trevor, was a lorry driver, not a lion-tamer. He was always buying things from blokes he met on the road, usually dodgy stereos or TVs that exploded after a week. But this box was different: it had air holes cut in it. Whatever was in this box needed to breathe!

The whole family crowded round as Danny pulled up the flaps.

"Softly!" said his dad. "We don't want to scare him. He's only a baby!"

Danny peeked into the box and recoiled in shock. A baby what?

Then the others were peering in.

"Aah!" said his mum.

"Oh, sweet!" said his sister, while Danny's brain did

somersaults inside his skull.

"Well?" said his dad. "It's for you Dan. Do you like it?"

"Wharrisit?" Danny asked.

"Oh, Danny!" said his mum.

"You moron!" said Sam.

"Dan, it's a puppy!" said his dad. "I thought that's what you always wanted."

"Yeah, yeah it was – I mean it is," said Danny. He was really confused now. He knew it must be a wind-up. His dad was always playing pranks on him. But how had he managed this? "I just meant, what sort is it?"

"Oh, well, you've got me there," said his dad. "A mongrel, I suppose. The bloke I got it off didn't seem to know either. Just wanted rid of it."

I'll bet he did, thought Danny.

His mum, Alison, was gazing into the box again. "It is hard to guess the breed," she agreed. "I mean it's sort of brown, sort of fluffy. It looks a bit like…"

"Like every dog you've ever seen rolled into one!" Sam finished for her.

Danny looked at the creature in the box. It looked like no dog he'd ever seen. He had seen brown dogs and black ones, white ones and yellow-golden ones; he had seen spotted ones, hairy ones, fluffy ones and smooth ones, but he had never before seen a purple, scaly one.

The creature opened one eye and then the other. They were golden-green, shiny as marbles, with a vertical slit of a pupil down the middle and they were looking straight at Danny, without blinking.

"Ah, look," said Sam, "He's waking up!" She began talking to the creature in a soppy voice, but it never took its eyes off Danny. He stared back, hypnotised, until finally it blinked: two grey, leathery eyelids swept in from the sides, like lift doors closing and opening. Danny started backwards with shock.

"Did you see that?" he demanded. "Did you see how it blinked?" He leaned in close to the creature. "You watch!" he told the others. "Go on," he told it. "Do it again! Blink!"

The creature cocked its head to one side, still staring unwaveringly at Danny.

"Blink," he coaxed, and it cocked its head the other way.

"Danny what is wrong with you?" asked his mum.

"He's mental, that's what!" said Sam.

"I thought you'd be pleased, Dan," said Trevor, "but if you don't want it…"

Danny looked up quickly. "I never said I didn't want it!" he said. "It's just…a bit of a surprise, that's all."

The creature was still curled up in the box, its long tail wrapped around its body, its leathery wings folded neatly across its back. Danny was almost sure now that it wasn't a wind-up; he didn't know what it was, but he thought he might as well start enjoying it.

"Thanks, Dad," he said, beaming suddenly. "It's great!"

His dad breathed a sigh of relief. "Mind you," he warned, "you'll have to look after him: feed him, walk him, clean up his messes!"

"I will, Dad, I promise," said Danny. "Can I take him up to my room?"

"Don't let it wee on the carpet," said his mum.

Up in his bedroom, Danny carefully examined his new pet. It was definitely purple, a metallic sort of purple, with other colours that moved across the surface, like petrol rainbows across a puddle. Sam would know the proper word: she was really good at art, but Sam, like his parents, thought the thing in the box was a brown furry puppy. It would be no use asking her to describe its wonderful colours. Danny couldn't understand it. He could clearly see it was a dragon. He had known it was a dragon from the moment he opened the box, but it seemed he was the only one who knew it.

"What is it?" he asked. "Magic? I don't believe in magic."

The dragon was watching his face again, its intelligent, golden-green eyes taking in a scruffy eleven-year-old with sticky-up hair and too many freckles.

Danny tried an experiment. "Blink," he said, but it did not blink. Instead it put its head on one side again.

"Blink," repeated Danny, softly, and the dragon's head tilted the other way. "You like that word, don't you?"

The dragon uncoiled itself and stood up, very slowly, inclining its head slightly in agreement.

"That's what I'll call you, then! Blink!" said Danny.

To show his approval, Blink jumped elegantly out of the box. He suddenly looked much bigger, his head on a level with Danny's as he knelt beside the box. Danny felt a brief ripple of fear pass through his belly, but he held his ground while the dragon came up and sniffed him with its long snout. Its breath felt warm on Danny's skin, and it stank like rotten eggs.

"We might have to get you some breath mints!" said Danny, coughing slightly.

Very slowly, he put out a hand and touched the dragon's scaly nose. It was cold, hard and leathery under his fingers. He moved his hand up to the top of the creature's head, feeling the huge, scaly ears and the rubbery, triangular ridge that sat just between them. The dragon stood very still as Danny moved slowly around it, looking it over. The ridges continued all the way down its back, getting larger in the middle, then smaller as they carried on down its tail.

It looked just like dragons look in storybooks, only smaller. It must have been a metre long from its flared nostrils to the magnificent, arrowhead tip of its tail. Its teeth and claws glinted fearsomely, but Danny was pleased to see it did not have horns. What it did have was an Elvis quiff, though not one made of hair, obviously. It was that first ridge, the one just between its ears, the way it flopped slightly forwards. The dragon caught Danny grinning at it and gave him a sideways glance that made him look away in a hurry.

"I wonder how old you are. Are you a baby or what?" Danny asked. In answer, the dragon stretched, proudly, extending his wings to their largest size. They were scalloped, like a bat's wings, and the skin was slightly see-through. They were also pathetically small for the size of its body.

"Can you fly with those little things?" Danny wondered out loud.

Blink fixed Danny with a steely gaze and then firmly turned his back on him. Danny knew at once that he should not have mentioned the wings. Dragons, it seemed, were easily offended.

"Sorry," he said. "I didn't mean anything by it. I expect they'll grow. Just like I'll grow some muscles one day!" Danny flexed his arms to show where the muscles should be. There was not even a bulge. His dad always said he had arms like soggy spaghetti. Blink turned a disdainful gaze on them and Danny hoped he'd been forgiven. Good job I didn't mention the quiff, he thought.

Blink began to explore Danny's room. He poked his nose into the cupboard and the chest of drawers, both standing open, as usual, with clothes overflowing out of them. He delicately put his front legs up on the chair so he could see on top of Danny's desk, sniffing at everything he could reach. Next, he poked his nose under the bed, emerging proudly with a cheese sandwich that Danny had dropped at least a week ago.

"I wouldn't eat that!" warned Danny, but he was too late. Blink swallowed the sandwich in one bite.

"Hungry, eh?" said Danny, and the dragon, in response, gave an almighty burp. Danny recoiled from the strong smell of bad eggs.

"I wonder what you do eat," he said. "Not fair maidens, I hope. That could be a bit of a problem!" He laughed nervously, before adding, "Mind you, you can eat our Sam any time you like!"

Blink was not listening: he was foraging again under the bed. This time he emerged with a pair of Danny's underpants on his nose.

"Ugh!" said Danny, lunging for the pants.

Blink was too quick. A flick of his head and the pants disappeared down his throat. Another huge burp erupted; this time Danny thought he saw a puff of smoke. Danny hastily stuffed things away and closed the drawers.

"You can't eat clothes!" he explained, but the dragon now had his head in the waste paper bin. He had found a Sherbet Fountain Danny had thrown away after it had become soggy. Blink swallowed it, liquorice, paper and all, eagerly licking the last traces off his nose with a long, black tongue. A cloud of sherbet billowed around him and he suddenly tossed his head back and gave a mighty sneeze. The contents of Danny's bin burst into flames.

"Hey watch it!" Danny leaped to his feet, looking around for water. He found a half-empty can of coke and poured that onto the fire. The flames went out, but the plastic bin was sagging, half-melted.

"How am I going to explain that to Mum?" wondered Danny, then he realised what had just happened. "You can breathe fire!" he added. "Cool!"

They couldn't stay in Danny's room forever. The outdoors had to be faced. Danny's first trip out with Blink was eventful to say the least. It started with the collar. His dad had stopped at a pet shop and bought a smart, red leather collar and a lead. He had also bought dog bowls, dog food, a brush (great, thought Danny, if only dragons had hair!) and a red, squeaky dog toy, shaped like a chicken. To Danny's horror, his dad poked the toy towards Blink's mouth. For a moment, Danny feared he might just melt it with a snort of fiery breath, but instead he took the toy disdainfully between his teeth. The roll of his eyes plainly said, 'This is beneath me, you know'.

"Look," said Trevor, "he's wagging his tail!"

Danny looked at Blink's tail, swishing majestically, like an angry tiger's. How his dad could see it as wagging, Danny could not understand, but he was beginning to realise where the magic lay. Somehow, when the others looked at Blink, they saw what they expected to see.

Blink wolfed down a bowl of dog food, followed by a large amount of water.

"Can I take him out?" Danny asked.

"Yes, but you must keep him on the lead," said Trevor. "Owning a dog is a big responsibility and we're placing a lot of trust in you." He glanced at Alison and Danny saw immediately what was going on. Mum and Dad logic went something like this: Danny tells lies and is not doing well in school; if we buy Danny a pet he'll have to take responsibility; he'll have to grow up and stop telling lies. Great logic, except for the one gaping hole. Somehow, Danny didn't know how, they had managed to get him a pet that was the very stuff of stories! He could have laughed out loud, but instead he bent down and tried to put the collar around Blink's neck. Blink tossed his head and growled a warning.

"Show him who's boss," said Trevor, firmly.

I know who's boss, thought Danny: the one with the enormous teeth and the fire-breathing capability! He tried again. "Please, Blink," he said, through gritted teeth. "Be a good puppy or we won't be allowed out!"

Blink got the message. This time he stood still and let Danny place the collar around his neck. It looked ridiculous and the red clashed terribly with the purple! Blink gave another toss of his head and the delicate, red collar changed into a thick black one with hefty silver spikes all round it. Blink looked enormously pleased with himself and Danny snorted with laughter.

"What's funny?" demanded Trevor.

"Nothing," said Danny, trying to control his giggles. "Can we go now?"

On the way to the park, Blink behaved just the way a puppy should. He pulled mercilessly on the lead, sniffed every smell and stopped to eat a few choice items off the pavement. Outside the chip shop, he made a beeline for the rubbish bin. It was one of those plastic ones with a solid top and large slots around the side to post rubbish into. Blink posted himself into it, his front half disappearing to leave just his bottom sticking out. Danny yanked on the lead, but to no avail. The dragon was strong.

The chip shop owner banged on the window and gestured at them, but fortunately he was too busy serving to come out. Several people stopped to watch and laugh and one old lady told them off, waving her umbrella. It was a full five minutes before the dragon re-emerged from the bin, licking his lips. He gave an enormous burp and a huge cheer erupted from the crowd. The chip shop man waved his fist at them and Danny dragged Blink wordlessly away.

The park was no better. It was full of kids who gathered round to admire the new puppy. There were lots of 'ooh's and 'aah's, but no one shouted dragon, so Danny relaxed a bit. It seemed the magic worked on everyone but him. Dogs, however, were not so easy to fool. A Yorkshire terrier ran at Blink, snarling and snapping, while a Rottweiler whimpered and cowered behind its owner's legs.

Danny turned and headed up the hill, where it was quieter. Blink disappeared into a thicket of bushes. Catching up, Danny heard digging. He poked his head into the bushes to see the dragon squatting over the hole he had dug. He shot Danny another of his wounded looks: clearly he did not wish to be disturbed. Danny mumbled an apology and stood as far away as the lead would allow. He had to: the smell of dragon dung was enough to make his eyes water. The dragon finished his business and filled in the hole.

They walked slowly around the park, Blink exploring every tree, bush and rubbish bin. By the time they came back to the play area, most of the children had gone home for tea. There was just a small boy, playing in the sandpit. Blink looked longingly at the swings and slides through the bright metal fence that was meant to keep dogs out. In fact, he shoved his head through the railings until Danny was sure he would get it stuck. He could just imagine calling the fire brigade. 'It's my dragon, you see. He's got his head stuck in some railings…' But Blink was not stuck, just smitten. Before Danny knew what had happened, the dragon had slipped his collar and jumped over the fence.

Danny scrambled after him. By the time he got inside, the dragon had climbed the steps of the slide and was sitting at the top, tail tucked around him, a look of sheer delight on his scaly face.

"Come down!" hissed Danny. "No, not that way!"

It was too late. Blink had whizzed down the slide, somersaulted off at the bottom and righted himself, shaking his head in astonishment. Danny lunged for him, but the dragon was already climbing the steps for another go. The little boy at the sandpit pointed and shrieked. His mother came striding towards Danny.

"Get your dog out of here!" she demanded. "You know they're not allowed!"

"Sorry," muttered Danny, blushing. "He's only a puppy. He don't know any better!"

Blink fixed the mother with an unwavering stare.

"Well, yes," she said, slowly, "I can see that now." She gazed fondly at Blink and started talking in that silly, high-pitched voice that women use to talk to babies. "He's a lovely puppy, aren't you boy? And so clever to climb all those steps!"

Her little son had followed her and was pointing at Blink, laughing delightedly. "Doddy! Look! Doddy on the slide!"

"Come here!" hissed Danny, and Blink finally came.

"Pretty doddy!" announced the toddler, patting Blink hard on the head with a fat, pink hand.

Danny forced a grin as he dragged Blink away. "You don't half know how to lay on the charm!" he complained, but he couldn't be more than a little cross with the dragon. "We'll come back later," he whispered, "when it's quiet."

After tea that evening, Danny kept his promise and returned to the playground. It was dark and all the little kids had gone home, so Blink was able to play to his heart's content. He slid down the slide over and over, chin up and wings outstretched. His oddly dignified expression made Danny laugh all the harder. Then the dragon jumped on and off the swings, sending them flying to and fro: he was lightning fast and his balance was excellent. Finally, Blink got on the roundabout and Danny whizzed it round. When the dragon got off he was too dizzy to walk straight. He bumped smack into the climbing frame and fell over backwards. Danny laughed until his sides ached.

"Silly doddy!" he said through his giggles.

Blink recovered from his dizziness, climbed to the top of the climbing frame and looked over the edge, flexing his wings.

"Careful, Blink!" called Danny. He still worried that those little wings might not hold the dragon up. He was right. Blink nose-dived off the climbing frame, landing in a crumpled heap on the ground. Before Danny could get to him, he was up the frame for another go. Ten tries later, Blink was falling no less heavily, and Danny thought he would be sick if he laughed any more.

That night, to Danny's amazement, his parents agreed to let Blink sleep in his room. Remembering the sneezing incident, Danny filled a couple of plastic bottles with water and put them under his bed, just in case. Blink crawled under there too, sending Danny's junk flying as he fashioned a den for himself.

"Oh, there are my football socks!" exclaimed Danny. "No, don't eat 'em!" Danny hastily shoved them into a drawer.

Blink gave him a disdainful stare as if he would never have considered eating socks.

The dragon settled in his den and Danny climbed into bed, feeling suddenly exhausted. He was just nodding off when a huge weight landed on his legs.

"Blink, what the hell are you doing?" Danny demanded, as he dragged his legs out from under the dragon. Blink did not respond: he had curled up and appeared to be deeply asleep. Danny shook his head. Dragons, he thought, there's no arguing with them.

He lay down in what remained of his bed and fell asleep with one hand on Blink's scaly neck.

3

Dragon-taming for Dummies

On Saturday morning Danny awoke with two miraculous thoughts: it was half-term and he had a pet dragon. He blinked and rubbed his eyes. That couldn't be right. That must have been a dream. He stretched out a cramped leg and felt a solid lump at the bottom of the bed. The lump woke up, jumped onto Danny's chest and licked Danny's face with a warm, smelly tongue. The clock said five thirty. By six o'clock, Danny was dressed and they were off on an adventure, taking as much food as they could carry.

That day, and every day that week, they walked for miles, over fields and through woods, by rivers and canals. Blink hunted rabbits and Danny tried not to hear him crunching them. The dragon needed to hunt: he was ravenously hungry all the time, and dog food did little to fill him up. Danny often shared his own food – his mum thought he must be having a growth spurt. And they got a free bone most days after Blink charmed the butcher with his cutest puppy impression.

What Blink liked most, though, was ice cream: mint choc chip was his favourite. If he had too much, he got a bit giddy, like Danny's mum when she had had too many glasses of wine. Danny loved to feed the dragon ice cream then take him to the playground and watch him fall off things.

Danny's parents were pleased with how well he was looking after his 'puppy'.

"It's good to see you out of the house and off your PlayStation," said Trevor.

Alison was amazed that the puppy never once messed indoors. "I can't believe how well house-trained he is!" she said.

Danny had to smile to himself when he thought of Blink's toilet habits. He was cleaner than any dog could ever be, probably cleaner than some humans!

By the end of the half-term holiday, Danny could not remember a time when he had not had a dragon. It seemed the most natural thing in the world. The week was over all too soon. Danny had to go back to school and Blink would be left alone all day. After much persuasion, Danny's mum agreed to let him come home at lunchtime. That way he could take Blink for a walk. It was quite a result for Danny: not only would he see Blink, but he would be spared that hour in the playground with Wayne Smith. And he would never have to share his lunch again, except, of course, with Blink.

On Monday morning, Danny was the last to leave the house. His mum made him shut Blink in the kitchen. Danny gave him extra rations for breakfast.

"No stealing food!" he lectured.

The dragon looked set to sulk at the very suggestion.

"I mean it!" said Danny. "The fridge and cupboards are out of bounds!"

As Danny walked into school, late, the first people he saw were Wayne and his cronies. He had been so busy worrying about Blink that he did not notice them until it was too late. There were five of them and they stood in a menacing huddle across the path. Between them they had five baseball caps, four earrings, one pierced eyebrow and no school bags. They seemed to be competing for who could have the shortest tie and the longest shirt tails. Wayne, of course, always won. If they had had a competition for the ugliest he would have won that too. With his shaved head and enormous ears, he was more like a monkey than most monkeys were. He had short legs, powerful shoulders and long arms like a cave man.

Danny was always vaguely surprised to see him walking on two legs.

"Pants-on-Fire!" Wayne greeted him, with a slap on the back that made Danny cough. Wayne grinned, revealing his missing front tooth. He had lost it in a fight. The other boy had lost three.

Danny glanced around the playground. Why was there never a teacher in sight when you needed one?

"Was you avoiding us in the holidays?" asked Wayne. "Only I thought you enjoyed our little chats!" His arm was round Danny's shoulder now, but it was more like a stranglehold than a gesture of friendship. "We've missed him, haven't we, boys?"

"I've missed his lunches," agreed a fat boy called Stephen, slapping his stomach and belching loudly.

"Yeah, let's have a look what he's got today," said Wayne, grabbing Danny's bag.

"I haven't got any lunch," Danny said, quickly. "I forgot it." He was not about to tell them he was going home for lunch in case they decided to come with him.

"Oh dear, you'll be hungry then, won't you?" said Wayne, beginning to empty Danny's rucksack anyway. "Where's your mobile phone, then?"

Danny remembered, with relief, that he had left it on the kitchen worktop in his hurry. "Haven't got one," he lied.

"Ahh. Can't Mummy and Daddy afford one? Does lion-taming not pay that well?"

The rest of the gang sniggered.

"Perhaps they think he'll phone people up and tell them lies!" said Tony, and they sniggered again. Tony was Wayne's second-in-command, and he was almost as stupid and ugly as Wayne. His hair was spiked with so much gel it was like glass. He could have used it as a weapon and most probably did.

Danny's cheeks burned with anger but he looked at the ground, determined to ignore them. I mustn't get in a fight, he told himself; I mustn't get kept in at lunchtime.

Wayne had just upended Danny's bag so that the last few things fell out on the path, when the deputy head, Mr Sergeant, rounded the corner. He was a very tall, skinny man who walked like a wind-up toy, stiff-legged, body rocking backwards and forwards. He crossed the playground in a few huge strides, bearing down on the little group.

"What do you boys think you're doing?" he demanded in his foghorn voice. He only had one volume setting: maximum. "It's after the bell, you know." He saw who it was. "Smith, is it? Up to no good, I expect."

"No, Sir," said Wayne, innocently. "Danny here dropped his bag and everything fell out. We was just helping him pick it all up, wasn't we, lads?"

The others grunted in agreement and began picking up Danny's possessions and handing them to him.

Mr Sergeant looked dubious. "Aren't we good citizens today?" he remarked with a sniff. "And what have you got to say for yourself, Squire? Have these lads been helping you?"

"Yes, Sir," Danny muttered, without looking up.

Sergeant sniffed again. "Right, well run along to classes, all of you."

Wayne and the others evaporated as Danny stuffed the last few things into his bag. Mr Sergeant gave one last enormous sniff and strode off, leaving Danny to scurry into class.

All morning, Danny tried to stay out of trouble, while his teachers made sarcastic comments about how quiet he was.

"Are you ill today, Squire?" enquired the maths teacher. "Only I've never seen you sit still for that long!"

At break Danny tried to keep himself to himself, but everyone wanted to know about his puppy.

"So that's why you never called for me in the holidays," said Jason. "I was right bored!"

"Sorry," Danny muttered, "I was busy with the dog." He felt a pang of guilt: he had never even given Jason a thought.

"Well, thanks for bringin' him round to show me! I thought we was mates." Jason shuffled off and wouldn't turn when Danny called him back.

When the lunch bell rang, Danny ran out of the school gates and all the way home. Blink was curled up innocently in his dog bed. Taking Danny's lecture to heart, he had opened neither fridge nor cupboards. He had, however, raided the dustbin. The kitchen floor was knee-deep in rubbish and the dragon looked extremely pleased with himself.

Danny was not so thrilled. "This means less time to play," he scolded.

Blink hung his head as Danny began picking up the rubbish. He even tried to help, picking bits up in his mouth to put into the bin bag, but most times he missed and Danny got angrier with him.

"Give over! You're making me slower!"

When it was all picked up, the kitchen floor was sticky. It would never do for Alison to see it like that. Reluctantly, Danny got out the mop.

Twenty minutes late, they headed to the park where Blink did his best to make Danny laugh. He hid in bushes and jumped out on Danny, or climbed trees and hung upside down like a giant bat. Danny found he could not stay angry. Dragons would be dragons, after all.

When his mum came home that evening, she was

pleasantly surprised: the kitchen was cleaner than she had left it!

"Danny, did you mop the floor?" she asked in consternation.

"Yeah, Mum, I thought I'd just help you out a bit!"

Owning a dragon proved to be one problem after another. No sooner had Danny sorted out his school routine than things began disappearing in the Squire household. Danny, of course, got the blame.

"What have you done with my watch?" Sam accused him. Sam was fourteen. She was a pain in the bum and she was always trying to get Danny in trouble.

"I've been wearing it to school," he replied. "I've always wanted a big, pink, shiny watch!"

"Oh, ha ha!" replied Sam.

A few days later, Alison lost her locket. It was gold, with pictures of both the children in it. Trevor had bought it for her fortieth birthday and she wore it every day, only taking it off to have a bath. Unlike Sam, she didn't accuse Danny but once or twice he caught her looking sideways at him.

Then Danny lost his front door key and his mum grounded him until he had searched his bedroom.

"What if you've dropped it outside somewhere?" she ranted. "Anyone could break into the house!"

"If I've dropped it outside, what's the point of

looking inside?" But his mum was in no mood for logic.

"You can tidy your room while you're in there!" she added, shoving a roll of bin bags into his hands.

Danny sighed. There was nothing he hated more than tidying his room. Reluctantly, he began picking up dirty clothes, food wrappers and smelly trainers. Blink sat on the bed, watching the proceedings with a beady eye. The dragon was always ready for a game. Danny sent his pyjamas flying up onto the bed and Blink picked them up in his mouth and sent them flying back.

"Give it a rest!" said Danny, peeling his pyjama bottoms from around his head. "If I don't find the key we won't be allowed out!"

The dragon huffed off to his den under the bed.

Sam poked her head round the door to smirk. "Oh, there *is* a carpet in here and it's *blue*! I'd completely forgotten!"

"Bog off, Sam," said Danny, without looking up.

It took an hour but finally the floor, bed and desk were clear. Danny had filled two bin bags with rubbish, some of which even he could not identify. There was still no sign of the key. He had tried every pocket, his school bag and sports kit. There was only one place left to look. Getting down on his hands and knees, Danny peered under the bed. Blink gave a warning hiss: this was his territory and he guarded it as fiercely as a small dragon could.

"I know," said Danny. "But I have to look."

He looked. It was more of a mess than he remembered. Blink had shredded a jumper to make his nest – the revolting, snot-green one that Gran had knitted Danny for Christmas.

"Cheers," said Danny. "I was wondering how to get rid of that!"

He reached in gently amongst the shreds of green wool. The little dragon became more agitated, rushing from side to side, making threatening lunges towards Danny. A tell-tale curl of smoke rose from his nostril.

"Calm down!" Danny soothed. "I'm not going to mess up your bed but I need to find my key!" As he said it, his fingers touched something hard and cold amongst the soft bedding. He pulled it out. It was not his door key. It was Sam's watch.

"You've got to be kidding!" said Danny. "What's this doing here?"

Blink hung his head.

"Have you had it all this time?" Danny continued. "You do know she'll kill me if she finds it in here. Why did you do it?"

The dragon turned away, sulking, while Danny continued the search. He pulled out a silver picture frame that should have been in his mum's bedroom.

How long had that been there? Not long enough for her to have missed it, thankfully. Further foraging produced a bottle opener, a pair of nail scissors, a few coins, his mum's precious locket and, finally, his door key.

Danny laid out all the shiny objects in a row while Blink looked alternately proud and displeased.

"What do you want with all this stuff?" Danny asked, and then it hit him. Treasure!

Every story told you that dragons hoard treasure. Blink had been trying to sleep on a pile of wealth. Danny tried hard not to smile as he looked at the pathetic collection. Apart from his mum's locket, none of it was at all valuable. Some treasure hoard!

"You mustn't take things," Danny tried to explain. "We'll get in trouble. They'll think it was me. We have to give them back." Danny could see the small dragon beginning to bristle with indignation, so he added, quickly. "You can keep these!" He shoved the nail scissors, bottle opener and coins back into the dragon's den. "We'll find you some more treasure, I promise."

Danny returned the picture frame to his mum's bedroom. The locket, he dropped into the dressing table drawer. Hopefully, his mum would think it had fallen in. The watch was trickier. He couldn't give it back to Sam; she'd only start accusing him again. In the end, he hid it behind the laundry bin in the bathroom. As he had hoped, his mum found it and told Sam off for being so careless. Danny allowed himself a little smile of satisfaction. It was always good to see someone else get into trouble, especially if that someone was Sam.

Danny's mum was really pleased with his room. She came bustling in with the hoover, and Danny had to grab it off her before she could find Blink's den.

"I'll do it!" he yelled.

"All right. What have you done with the real Danny?" she asked, but she left him to it, smiling. "You are growing up!" she remarked.

Danny sighed. From now on he would have to hoover his own room.

"You're hard work, you are!" he complained to Blink, but even as he said it, Danny knew the dragon was worth it.

Next day, Danny took his pocket money and went, self-consciously, to a charity shop in town. He left Blink tied up outside while he bought the cheapest, gaudiest jewellery he could find.

The old lady behind the counter gave him a funny look.

"It's for a school play," he told her, with a reassuring grin.

Back at home he offered the treasures to Blink, but the dragon turned his nose up as if he had never seen

31

such rubbish. Danny could not understand it: they looked much better to him than old keys and nail scissors. He stuffed them crossly into his bottom drawer, muttering about ungrateful dragons. The next day, they had disappeared into the nest under the bed. Of course, thought Danny, treasure had to be taken, not given as a present.

From then on, Danny kept his eyes peeled for treasure. When his dad took him to car boot sales, he always spent a few pence on something shiny. Then he hid it in his room. It always disappeared in a matter of days. Soon the den under the bed was so full of treasure that Blink could not fit into it. He had to sleep on Danny's bed every night, which was very comfortable for one of them, at least.

4

Trouble in the Park

Danny should have known that trouble was brewing when a bush in the park started talking to him one evening.

He was at the top of the hill and Blink was off in the undergrowth somewhere.

"Psst!" said the bush.

Danny turned, saw no one and decided he'd imagined it.

"Psst!" said the bush again, and then, "Over here, Daniel!"

This time Danny's head whipped round. He hadn't imagined it: someone had said his name. "Who's there?" he called in the direction of the talking bush.

A face appeared between two branches. For a moment Danny thought it was an owl: the eyes were so big behind the thick glasses. But no, it was an old man, a nutter most likely. Danny hung back, in case he had no trousers on: you never could tell with nutters in the park.

"Can anyone see us?" asked the old man, his owl eyes glancing wildly around.

Danny looked. There was no one about, but he wasn't going to admit that. He knew about stranger danger, and this man was certainly strange. "There are two blokes with an Alsatian coming up the hill," he lied smoothly.

"Keep an eye on them," the old man instructed. "Let me know if they come near. We must talk quickly." He spoke very fast, clipping all the words short, and he had an odd accent, American, Danny thought.

"Sorry, mate, I haven't really got time to chat today!" said Danny, starting down the hill and calling for Blink.

"But it's about the dragon!" hissed the man in the bush.

Danny backtracked. "Did you say dragon?" He found he, too, was looking around now, as if someone might be listening.

"That's right."

"But how did you…?"

"Oh, I know what he is all right."

The man took a couple of steps forward and Danny was relieved to see that he was wearing trousers. They were khaki, camouflage pattern. So were his shirt and his waistcoat (one of those with pockets all over, like fishermen wear). Even his baseball cap was khaki. He looked like a short, fat, aging commando. He had a long, grey, straggly beard and a grey pigtail that stretched all the way down his back. As nutters in the park went, this one could win prizes. And yet he had said dragon…

"Who are you?" Danny asked, still keeping a safe distance.

"My name's Vale," the man replied. A hand appeared out of the bush for Danny to shake. Danny ignored it and the hand quickly disappeared. "Professor Vale. I'm a rocket scientist, at least I used to be."

"Yeah, and I'm a brain surgeon!"

Vale cackled. "You're a funny boy. Your dad said you were."

"You know my dad?" asked Danny, warily. As if that wasn't the oldest trick in the book.

Vale did not answer. Instead he asked, "Are you keeping an eye on our Alsatian-walking friends?"

"Oh," said Danny, pretending to look. "They've stopped about halfway up. One of them's smoking a fag."

Vale nodded.

"You talk funny! Where do you come from?" Danny asked.

"Well, a long time ago I was Canadian," replied the man. "But my quest has taken me just about everywhere."

"Quest?" asked Danny. "What are you? A knight?"

"I'm a dragon-hunter!" Vale replied, then seeing Danny's expression he added. "I don't hurt them, I just study them."

Danny gaped at the odd little man. "Are you one of them loonies off the Internet? Them ones what think dragons really exist." Danny had seen the websites. Mad, the lot of them.

Vale chuckled. "You know they exist!"

"Well…"

"Or did you think he was the only one?"

"I… yeah, I s'pose I did really. So… are there loads of them?"

"I wouldn't say loads, exactly, but I've come across a few in my travels."

Danny found he was gaping again. He didn't know what to say. To his enormous relief, Blink finally appeared. Seeing the old man, he puffed himself up and gave a warning growl. Vale stepped forwards, out of the bushes. Blink put his head on one side and then the other.

"Come on, boy," said Vale. He crouched down and waited, one hand outstretched.

Blink took a step towards the man, sniffing. He paused, sniffed again. Finally, he went up and nuzzled his snout into Vale's outstretched hand. Vale gently patted Blink's head, then tickled him behind the ears, just the way he liked it.

Danny felt a stab of jealousy. "How come he knows you?" he demanded.

"Where do you think you got him from?" asked Vale, smiling.

"My dad got him from some old bloke he met on the road…" Suddenly Danny put two and two together. "You? But… how? Why?"

Vale immediately began glancing around again. "Because they're following me. I think they know. It's not safe for you to be seen talking to me. I've already been here too long." He glanced down the hill. "Where are those Alsatian-walkers? Oh, I see. You had me going." And he gave another chuckle and stepped back into the bushes. "Smart boy!"

"Wait!" said Danny. "How do I get in touch with you?"

"You don't!" said Vale. "Be vigilant, Daniel. They could be anywhere!"

"Who could?" asked Danny but the old man was gone.

Danny walked around the clump of bushes and saw him skulking from tree to tree down the hill. He couldn't have looked more conspicuous if he'd tried.

"Mad as lettuce!" Danny pronounced, shaking his head. He turned to Blink. "Is he your daddy?"

The dragon raised his head to its haughtiest level and stalked away down the path.

Danny was a bit jumpy for the next few days, looking over his shoulder to see if he was being followed, which of course he wasn't. Be vigilant, Vale had said. Vigilant for what? Who were 'they' and why were they following the old man? Danny decided the Professor was paranoid. The trouble was that paranoia was infectious. Once or twice he did have the feeling he was being watched. An old lady stopped them and asked a lot of questions about Blink. What breed was he? How old? Where had he come from? Danny answered politely, but vaguely. She was probably just lonely, after all. Then there was a man who looked at Blink in an odd way, a powerfully-built man, with a shaved head, a dark beard and a lot of tattoos. His black T-shirt bore the name of a heavy metal band and he looked like he could be their roadie. Danny knew you shouldn't judge people on looks but, as the man approached them, he instinctively put a hand on Blink's collar. He could feel that the dragon had tensed up, too. Then the man spoke.

"You seen a Rottweiler, son?" he asked in a rough, cockney voice. "Little bleeder's run off again!"

Danny shook his head. "Sorry, mate."

The man looked at Blink in that odd way again, narrowing his eyes, as though he was very short-sighted.

"That's a handsome dog you've got there."

"Thanks," replied Danny.

The man held out a hand, just as Vale had done. "Come here, boy!"

Blink stayed right where he was.

"I'd watch him, if I were you," warned Danny. "He can be a bit nasty with strangers." He made sure he emphasised the last word.

"Can he now?" asked the man, coolly. He withdrew his hand, but not before Danny had noticed a tattoo on the inside of his forearm, near the wrist. He thought it was an odd place to have one; surely it had been painful to have it done.

The tattooed man gave Blink another appraising look and sauntered off without another word.

Danny couldn't say why he was rattled by the incident. He had a couple of nightmares about tattooed men, but they were just dreams, weren't they?

The days went by and the nightmares stopped. Danny saw no more strange people or talking bushes and gradually, he forgot to be vigilant. In fact, he and Blink became more daring. As the winter nights got colder and darker, they had the playground to themselves most evenings. Blink could do a double somersault off the swings now, could come down the slide backwards, forwards, sideways and upside down. His acrobatics on the climbing frame would have won an Olympic medal. Most nights, he and Danny dared each other into stupid stunts. One evening, they were hanging upside down from the monkey bars, pulling faces at each other to see who would fall off first from laughing. They were having so much fun that Danny wasn't keeping a look-out. By the time he noticed, it was too late: they were surrounded.

"Well look who it is!" said Wayne Smith.

"Pants-On-Fire!" shouted Tony.

"And he's got a little friend!" finished Wayne.

Danny turned right way up and dropped warily to the ground; Blink landed lightly beside him. The boys closed the circle around them, waiting for the entertainment to start. Most of them were even more stupid than Wayne, and that was saying something. But they were big and strong and would attack on Wayne's command. Danny tensed, looking instinctively for a gap he could squeeze through. If he was quick he could sometimes get away from them.

"What sort of dog is that, then?" asked Wayne, looking closely at Blink.

Danny did not answer.

"Only I never saw a dog hang upside down!" said Wayne. "Are you training him for the circus?"

The others laughed.

"Perhaps he's an Australian dog," suggested Tony.

"Yeah, perhaps he's part dingo!" said Wayne.

You're part dingo, thought Danny, but he managed not to say it out loud.

"Dirty little runt, in't 'e?" said Tony.

"Ugly too," added Wayne.

"Not as ugly as you!" This time Danny had said it out loud.

Two of Wayne's thugs grabbed Danny and he braced himself for the attack, but Wayne did not give the order, not yet. Instead he turned on Blink with a mischievous glint in his eye.

"Let's see him do some more tricks, shall we?" he said, and he reached out to pick Blink up.

It happened in a flash. One minute Blink was cowering on the ground, doing his best puppy impersonation, the next he was halfway up the climbing frame, wings extended as far as they would go. His bared teeth glinted in the moonlight, and he let out a roar that scared even Danny. Wayne's thugs loosened their grip and Danny wriggled free. The gang backed away but Wayne himself seemed rooted to the spot, pointing a finger at Blink and making little whimpering noises. A tell-tale curl of smoke rose from Blink's nostril.

"No, Blink, not that!" hissed Danny, and Blink snarled in frustration and lashed out with his claws instead.

Wayne screamed, fell to the ground and scrambled

backwards, clutching his bleeding arm. "What he do that for? What kind of vicious dog you got there?"

Wayne's gang had scattered and some were already quite a distance away, but two of the braver ones stepped forward and pulled Wayne up, still screaming over his shoulder as he retreated, "He wants drowning, that dog. I'll get him. You wait, Squire!"

At that, Blink let out a jet of flame that washed across their three backsides. The boys screamed and ran faster than ever, patting at their smouldering jeans as they went.

Danny got the joke. "Now whose pants are on fire?" he shouted, throwing back his head and laughing. He felt braver than he had ever felt in his life. "Come and get us any time!" he called after them. "We'll be waiting!"

Blink was already back on the ground, carefully cleaning his claws as if to remove all traces of Wayne Smith. He looked extraordinarily pleased with himself. Danny scratched his ears affectionately. "That was amazing!" he said.

They set out for home, still laughing at their cleverness but, halfway there, Danny's legs began to shake. He felt suddenly weary. It had occurred to him that Wayne could make trouble. What if he told everyone that Blink had bitten him? Dogs could be put down for biting. What could Danny say to defend him when Wayne had a great big gash on his arm? Danny crawled miserably into bed where he tossed and turned all night, while Blink was buffeted like a ship on a stormy sea.

5

Pants on Fire!

The following day, Wayne was absent from school, and Tony made a throat-cutting gesture at Danny across the playground.

That evening, it seemed Danny's fears would be realised. His dad answered a knock at the door and Danny peered around him at an angry-looking man. He was as wide as he was tall, his hair cropped so short that it was little more than bristles. He reminded Danny of a grizzled, old chimpanzee he had once seen at the zoo. Danny knew in an instant that this man was related to Wayne Smith.

"Need a word with you about your boy's dog," the man growled. "Needs putting to sleep, that thing! Have you seen what it done to my son?"

He stepped aside to reveal Wayne, his arm heavily bandaged and a defiant smirk on his face.

Danny's heart sank.

"Are you saying our dog bit your son?" asked Trevor,

looking round questioningly at Danny.

"Bit him?" shouted Mr Smith. "He nearly took his bloody arm off!"

"Are you sure?" asked Trevor. "He's just a puppy, you know. He's only got baby teeth!"

Danny forced back a smile.

"Baby teeth?" said the man. "You should see Wayne's arm. We're after compensation!"

"Of course you are!" said Trevor, a glint of amusement in his eye.

"If you don't take this serious, we'll call the police!" threatened Mr Smith.

Danny's dad remained perfectly calm. "Danny, bring Blink here would you?"

Danny went to the kitchen and fetched Blink out. "Be nice!" he warned him as they approached the front door.

Blink cowered, trying to look harmless.

Mr Smith looked doubtful. "Is this the dog?" he demanded of Wayne.

"It looked bigger last night," muttered Wayne.

"Danny, do you know anything about this?" asked Trevor.

"No, Dad," replied Danny.

Wayne narrowed his eyes at Danny.

"Right, Wayne, show 'em your arm!" commanded Mr Smith, and he grabbed Wayne's arm and started scrabbling at the bandages.

"Ow! Dad!" said Wayne. "Gerroff! I'll do it!"

He began undoing the bandage and Danny glanced nervously at Blink. They were not out of the woods yet. Blink did not meet Danny's gaze: instead he fixed Wayne's arm with an unwavering stare. When the bandages were off, Mr Smith thrust his son's arm at them.

"Well?" he enquired. "What do you say to that, then?"

"I'd say your son's a very fast healer," observed Trevor.

Mr Smith turned Wayne's arm over, incredulous. There was not a mark on it.

"I don't understand," said Mr Smith. "There were a great big cut there last night. Ten stitches he had to have!"

He dropped Wayne's arm and Wayne looked at it stupidly, as if it did not belong to him.

"What have you done?" Mr Smith demanded of Wayne.

"Me, Dad? I ain't done nothin'!"

Mr Smith grabbed the arm again, turning it over and back again, rolling the sleeve up further as if the injury might somehow have moved. He even grabbed the other arm and inspected that, as if he thought the doctors had bandaged the wrong one. Danny had to bite his lip.

Wayne was in a panic now, scrabbling at his arm. "It's still there, Dad: I can feel it! It hurts!" But Mr

Smith was no longer listening. He was backing down the steps, pulling Wayne with him.

"You ain't heard the last of this!" he threatened.

"I think we have!" replied Trevor. As he swung the door shut, Danny could hear Wayne protesting and his dad swearing all the way down the street. Wayne was really going to catch it when he got home. For a moment Danny actually felt sorry for him, but only for a moment.

"Charming family," said Trevor, winking. "You can see where the son gets his good looks from, can't you?"

"Thanks, Dad," grinned Danny. "You were great!"

"Well, you and the pup played your parts well, too," said his dad. "You know I would swear that dog knows just when to be small and cute…"

"Tell me about it…"

Back in his room, Danny said to Blink, "What did you do to his arm? There wasn't a mark on it!" It always amazed him how many tricks the dragon had up its sleeve.

Blink was growing very quickly. Everyone commented on it. He could hardly turn round in the Squire's small kitchen.

"He's a good advert for my bones!" pronounced the butcher.

Danny had no idea how big the dragon would grow. What if he got too big for the house? Would people still believe he was a dog when he was bigger than Danny?

There was another worry, too. Blink's wings had doubled in size and no longer looked so ridiculous. When he jumped off the climbing frame he could glide a bit. He might very soon take off and fly and even Danny didn't know how he would explain a flying dog.

One night Danny woke to find his bedroom freezing cold. The window was wide open and Blink was missing. Danny poked his head out but there was no sign of the dragon in the garden or the street. Then a noise from above made Danny look up. There was Blink on the roof, flexing his wings.

"Blink, no!" said Danny, in the loudest whisper he dared, but Blink took no notice. He dived off the roof, spiralling beautifully in the air before plummeting, with a crash, into the dustbins.

Dogs began barking up and down the street; windows opened and heads poked out.

"Danny, shut that dog up!" called his dad, sleepily.

"Sorry, Dad," said Danny, as he sneaked down the stairs to let Blink in through the back door. "That was smart!" Danny told him. "How were you planning to get back in? Walk up the wall?"

Blink gave him a haughty stare as he stalked by on his way back to the bedroom.

"Dragons!" muttered Danny, slamming the window shut and locking it.

A few days later, Blink took off from the climbing frame and went up instead of down. He was immensely pleased and practised again and again until it was past curfew time. Danny's mum was furious. She grounded them for several days and Blink got so frustrated that he ate three trainers and half the coffee table. Danny's mum had to give in and let them out: she couldn't afford to lose any more furniture. After that the dragon practised flying every evening. Before long, he was able to take off from the ground, spiralling higher and higher until Danny lost sight of him in the darkness.

Left below, Danny kicked stones around aimlessly. He couldn't join in with this new game.

Then one Sunday afternoon, when the park was full of people, Blink left the ground in broad daylight.

"Blink, no!" hissed Danny. "Someone'll see!" But Blink took no notice, soaring away from him.

Danny stood, mesmerised. He had never seen Blink fly before – it had always been dark. It was beautiful, watching him swoop and dive. For a minute, Danny forgot to be afraid, but a shrill voice brought him back to earth with a bump.

"Mummy, look at that!"

Danny turned to see a small boy looking and pointing, his mother squinting up at the sky. Then they looked at Danny.

"Is that yours?" asked the mother.

"Is what mine?" His heart was thumping.

"The kite!" she said, pointing upwards. "You are flying it, aren't you?"

"Kite?" repeated Danny. He looked down at his hands, astonished to see that he was holding a kite string where moments before there had been a dog lead. Relief and wonder flooded in. Blink's magic had saved them again. Danny laughed like a loon. "I am flying it, aren't I?"

The woman gave him a look. "Can I ask where you got it? Only Tom, here, would love one. He loves dragons, don't you, Tom?"

The little boy nodded, never taking his eyes off Blink.

"Me too!" said Danny, still grinning like a half-wit.

"So where did you get it?" repeated the woman.

"I, er, dunno," he muttered. "It was a present."

"Oh, I see," she said, disappointed.

"Yeah, my uncle brought it back," Danny added, recovering. "From abroad. He travels a lot. On business."

The woman nodded. "Yes, it looks foreign," she pronounced. "Well it's a beauty, at any rate. You're a lucky lad."

"Yeah, I am!" agreed Danny. And I'm going to kill that dragon when he lands, he thought.

The mother had to drag her son back down the hill, his head craned round all the while to look at Blink. The dragon went on flying for a long time, spiralling and swooping and diving, and Danny could enjoy watching him, now he knew they were safe. When Blink eventually landed beside Danny, he wore an extremely smug expression.

"Very clever," said Danny, dryly. "I wish you could warn me when you were going to pull a stunt like that!"

Blink shook his wings haughtily and set off down the hill. Danny followed, realising he was once again holding a dog lead.

"Kite!" he muttered to himself. "Brilliant!"

He was so elated as he walked down the hill that he did not notice a figure standing quietly amongst the trees, a large figure with a bald head, a dark beard and a great deal of tattoos. As Danny passed, the man turned and walked away in the opposite direction, pulling a mobile phone from his pocket as he did so.

6

The Prize

Life in the Squire household was never dull. There was usually some kind of argument going on. As spring came round, they began to plan their summer holiday and the arguments got more heated than ever. Sam was desperate to go abroad, somewhere hot like Greece or Majorca. Last year they had gone to Cyprus, but now Danny had Blink to think of. "I can't take him abroad and I'm not leaving him behind!" he announced.

"There are kennels, Dan," his dad pointed out.

"Yeah, but they're really expensive, and how do we know they'll take proper care of him?" argued Danny. Kennels were, of course, out of the question.

"Dan, you're too indulgent with that dog," said Trevor.

"Well, he's special," Danny replied. "You have no idea how special," he added under his breath.

"Couldn't one of your school friends have him?" his mum suggested. Like Sam, she was keen to go abroad.

Danny shook his head, quickly making up excuses: one of his friends had allergies, another lived in a flat, a third had vicious dogs of his own…

"All right, all right!" his mum interrupted. "We'll think of something else."

"You lot go," said Danny. "Blink and I can go to Gran's."

"Out of the question!" said his mum. "Your gran's too old to cope with either of you, let alone both!"

"Then we stay in this country and take the dog with us," suggested Trevor.

Good old Dad, thought Danny. He wilted in hot weather and hated foreign food.

"Great!" said Sam, "We can take the rain with us too!"

The rows went on.

It was during this time that Danny saw Professor Vale again. It was a mild evening towards the end of April and Danny was at the top of the hill, Blink flying overhead, when a bush behind him said, "Psst!"

Danny only jumped a little this time. "Hello Professor!" he said, starting towards to the bush.

"Don't come over here!" hissed Vale. "Keep looking the other way!"

Danny rolled his eyes. "There's no one around!"

"Anything to report?" asked the bush.

"Nothing out of the ordinary," replied Danny. He told Vale briefly about the holiday dilemma.

"Holiday?" repeated the Professor, as if he never heard the word before. "I'm not sure that's a good idea!"

"Don't worry, we probably won't end up going anywhere," replied Danny. "We'll just spend all summer arguing about it! Where have you been, anyway? I haven't seen you for months."

"I've been here and there. I've got research to do, instruments to watch."

"Any more dragon sightings?" asked Danny.

Vale shook his head. He had come out of the bushes now, dressed in his usual camouflage gear.

Together they watched Blink fly.

"What a privilege!" muttered Vale.

Danny knew just what he meant. He never tired of watching.

"Did you know that other people see a kite?"

"Really?" asked Vale. "That's ingenious!"

"How does he do that? Change what people see?" Danny asked. It was one of the things that most intrigued him, and he thought Vale might know the answer.

"I'm not entirely sure," replied Vale, "but as far as I can tell they've developed a sort of highly-charged energy around them, that somehow distorts our perceptions."

"Like a force field?" asked Danny.

"More elaborate than that. Something that bends the laws of physics almost to breaking point," replied Vale. "I'm a scientist, as you know, and I've studied these things extensively. I think there's only one technical term you can apply to it."

"What's that?"

"Magic!" Vale's eyes twinkled and Danny laughed aloud.

"Yeah," he agreed. "That's what I thought it was!"

They watched Blink fly in companionable silence. It was good just being with someone who saw a dragon up there and not a kite.

"I think seeing them comes down to open-mindedness," Vale continued. "People who expect to see a dragon can see them, but most people have no expectation of seeing a dragon, so they see something easier for their brains to cope with. Like a dog…"

"I wasn't expecting to see a dragon," Danny pointed out.

"Well, no. You can see him because he lets you!"

"Same with you?"

"Not quite. You see I was there when he hatched out of his egg…"

"No way! What happened?"

"Another time," said Vale, stepping back into his bush.

Danny saw what had spooked him – two ladies with dogs coming up the path.

"It's OK, Professor, I know them," said Danny, but the bush was empty. Vale had already gone.

"No!" said Danny. He had not asked half the questions he had wanted to.

A couple of days after Danny's meeting with the Professor, his dad came off the phone with a huge grin on his face.

"I've only gone and won us a holiday!" he announced. That afternoon, Trevor had been approached by a salesman in the street. He had put his name down for a holiday brochure and been entered in a prize draw.

"And he's just phoned to say I won! Me! I've never won anything in my life!"

"That's great, Trev!" said Alison. "What's the holiday?"

"It's in Scotland!" Trevor enthused. "A holiday camp in the woods, by a lake. There's fishing, boating, windsurfing, bike tracks, a swimming pool: everything's included! And we're staying in a log cabin!"

"Brilliant!" said Danny. It sounded perfect for Blink.

Alison was pleased too. Now the arguments could stop.

They told Sam as soon as she came in.

"Fantastic! Where are we going?" she asked. Her face didn't so much fall as plummet when they told her.

"Scotland?" she moaned. "Bagpipes, shortbread, men in kilts?"

"No," said her dad, "beautiful scenery, fresh air and fun!"

"It sounds great, Dad," Danny reassured him.

"Great for you and your stupid dog," retorted Sam. "Why do we always have to do what Danny wants? It's not fair! I hate this family!" she shouted, and ran off to her room, slamming the door for good measure.

Danny didn't care: he was as excited as his dad was about the holiday. They spent the next few weeks making sure all the bikes were up to scratch, digging out fishing gear, cleaning and mending. His dad even bought him a sharp new penknife. Danny was thrilled.

"Boys together!" said Alison, rolling her eyes.

It never occurred to Danny what a coincidence it was, winning a holiday just when they needed one.

Danny did not see Vale again until July. It was a sultry evening just before the end of term and they were not in the park, but out near the river. The place was quite deserted, but Danny had nothing to fear from the Professor.

Vale was dressed in khaki. Danny got the impression he never wore anything else. He took off his cap to scratch his head, and Danny saw that he was quite bald on top, despite the long grey plait that hung down his back. Danny looked away, stifling a grin.

"I've got to go north again," said Vale. "You might not see me for a while."

"I think I can probably cope!" replied Danny.

"Don't be cheeky!" said Vale. "You need to stay vigilant. There are people out there who would take him from you at a moment's notice!"

"What people?" asked Danny.

"Believe it or not," Vale began, "you and I are not the only people mad enough to believe in dragons!"

"I don't believe in…" Danny began, and then bit his lip as Vale gave him a look.

"There are people who would use dragons for more sinister purposes."

"Like what?"

"Well, think, Daniel. Where there are dragons, what else must there be?"

"Dragon dung?" suggested Danny. He hated guessing games.

Vale did not smile. "Well, yes, but also?"

"Upturned bins? Chewed table legs? Piles of bones?"

"Piles of treasure!" finished Vale.

"Treasure?" echoed Danny. "Of course!" He thought of Blink's pathetic collection of shiny things under the bed. "That actually does make sense," he added.

"Yes, I like to make sense now and then, just to keep you guessing," said Vale, with a wry smile. "I'd like you to have a way of contacting me, just in case," he added, thrusting an old, dog-eared business card at Danny.

'Professor R D Vale, PhD' it said, with an address in Santa Monica, California.

"Of course, I don't live there any longer, so the address and phone number are useless," said Vale.

"Right," said Danny slowly, wondering what use the card was.

"The mobile number works," Vale explained.

"OK. Thanks," said Danny, making to pocket the card.

"But you mustn't use it. Unless it's a dire emergency. Phones can be tapped!"

Danny looked at the card again and sighed. There was an email address, scribbled on by hand. "Can I use that?" he asked.

"Yes you can," Vale replied, "but not too often. And don't call me Professor. Call me Uncle Rupert." He winked.

"Rupert?" echoed Danny. "Is that your name?" He looked at the initial R on the card.

"Don't be silly," replied Vale.

"Me?" asked Danny, but Vale ignored his sarcasm.

Pointing to Blink, he continued, "We'll call him the Research Project."

Mad as a bucket of custard, thought Danny.

"And you can sign yourself Davina."

"Davina?" That was going too far. "Why do I have to be Dav-?"

But Vale was gone again, leaving Danny holding the grubby card. Danny looked around and saw what had spooked him. A smartly-dressed, blond man was coming along the path, swinging a dog lead.

"Evening," said the man, showing a lot of white teeth as he smiled. "Nice dog!"

"Thanks," replied Danny, hastily stowing the card in his pocket. He looked around for the stranger's dog, so he could say something nice in return, but there was no dog in sight so he and Blink continued on their way home.

Danny had meant to tell Vale about the holiday. He felt sure the old man would want to know, but he always disappeared before Danny could really talk to him. After a week of indecision, he decided to use the email address.

'Dear Uncle Rupert,' he typed, raising his eyebrows as he did so. 'Thanks for all your help on my research project – it's going fine! I won't be in touch for a week because I'm going on holiday, but after that I'll look forward to hearing from you again, love, Davina.'

He sent the message and received no reply.

Next day they were off to Scotland. The journey would take at least four hours, his dad warned them. The car was piled with luggage; bikes on the back and other gear lashed to the roof rack. Blink suffered in a cage in the boot and Danny suffered in the back seat with Sam. She held him personally responsible for the fact that she was missing a foreign holiday, and sulked, loudly, the whole way there. She also managed to take up almost the whole of the back seat, so that Danny could never get comfortable. He was relieved when they made a lunch stop so he could stretch his legs.

Danny was walking Blink around the edge of the service station when a nearby shrub said, "Psst!"

"No way!" said Danny. He approached the shrub nervously. It was only a metre high: if Vale was in there he must be bent double! "Please tell me you're just an ordinary talking plant!"

"No, it's me," said Vale. "Down here!"

Danny looked both ways to check no one was watching, and then crouched down pretending to tie his shoelace. "What are you doing here?" he hissed at the bush.

"Making sure you're all right," Vale replied. "So, where are we going?"

"Well, *I'm* going on holiday to Scotland," replied Danny. "I have no idea where *you're* going!"

"I thought I'd tag along, make sure you're safe. Whereabouts in Scotland?"

Danny told him about the holiday.

"I don't like it," said Vale.

"You should talk to my sister!"

"You say your dad won it?"

"That's right!"

"It sounds fishy to me. If they know about the Orkney Islands, we could be playing right into their hands."

"What about the Orkney Islands?" asked Danny.

"That's where I found him!"

"There are dragons in the Orkney Islands?" said Danny in plain disbelief.

"Oh yes. There are over seventy islands, most of them uninhabited. Plenty of places to hide."

"Well, we're not going to the Orkneys," said Danny. "We're just going to a nice family campsite."

Danny was tired and cross from the journey. He didn't need Vale's paranoia on his holiday.

"They could be following you," Vale warned.

"The treasure people?"

Vale nodded. "They follow me!"

"Then why are you here?" Danny blurted out. "If they're following you, you might lead them straight to me!"

"Oh," replied Vale. "I hadn't thought of that!"

Danny sighed. For a smart person, the Professor could be really thick sometimes. "No offence, Professor, but I think we can manage without you for a week!" And he walked away without looking at the bush again.

As soon as they arrived at the holiday park, Danny forgot all about Vale and his suspicions. It was great – all pine forest and lakes. The log cabin was clean and homely, with a proper bathroom and kitchen. It only had two bedrooms, but Danny and Blink would be sleeping outside in Danny's two-man tent. More of a one-man-and-a-dragon tent, really, thought Danny.

On arrival, Sam disappeared to check out the pool, while Danny stayed to help unpack the car.

"Are you just going to let her go, Trev?" Danny's mum asked.

"Ali, I'm too hot and too tired to argue!" replied his dad.

Danny was hot and tired too, and Blink needed some exercise, but he stayed and put up his tent.

Sam returned an hour later when the tent was up and the dinner cooking. Danny rolled his eyes when he saw her wave goodbye to a group of teenagers, mostly boys. She inspected the cabin in the way a princess might inspect a sewage farm.

"Bit basic, isn't it?" was all she would say. "At least I don't have to sleep with that creature!" she conceded at last, nodding at Blink.

"Funny," said Danny. "That's just what he said about you!"

They ate outside at their own picnic bench. Sam moaned about everything: it was cold; the midges were biting her; the sausages were burnt and the potatoes were raw.

"You can cook tomorrow night, then!" said Alison. "And by the way, you're washing up this lot."

"What? But I said I'd meet up with the gang!"

"You just met them," said her mum, "and you are only fourteen."

"That's what you always say," complained Sam. "It's not fair! You treat me like a baby!"

"Can I take Blink for a run?" asked Danny, sensing a row brewing.

His dad nodded and Danny beat a hasty retreat. As he reached the woods, he could still hear Sam. "Great! Let *him* go on his own. And he's two years younger than me."

"But he's not alone," said his mum. "He's got the dog with him!"

"And we all know it's a killer!" added his dad, with a laugh.

If you only knew, thought Danny, smugly.

The woods stretched for miles and had wide paths cut through them. Blink bustled this way and that, exploring all the new smells. The hunting was good, judging by the squealing and crunching sounds that came from the undergrowth. They reached the lake just as the sun was setting over it. It was deserted, canoes and rowing boats piled up on the shore. Danny skimmed stones while Blink explored the little beach, then the dragon took off and flew over the water, swooping with great joy. Danny, wishing he could join in, ran in giant circles on the sand, arms out, as if they were wings. He knew it was childish, but it felt almost as good as flying.

7

Tattoo!

It was the best holiday Danny had ever had. Sam was wrong about the weather: it was hot and sunny all week. And Vale was wrong about the danger: they were safe as houses, or at least log cabins. Danny and Blink explored the woods or played by the lake. Danny swam while Blink remained on the beach, looking baleful. He hated water and would not put so much as a claw in the lake.

Danny bought a Frisbee from the campsite shop and it became their favourite game. Blink never missed catching it in his mouth.

"Blimey, Dan," said his dad, "That dog can almost fly!"

After that, Danny had to be careful not to throw the Frisbee too high.

Trevor and Danny tried windsurfing and canoeing. Sam tried to make the lifeguard notice her. Alison sat in a lounger, reading book after book. Everyone was having a good time.

Blink drew admiring glances from other holidaymakers. Everyone asked what breed he was and Trevor would laugh and say 'Heinz 57' which was his joke way of saying Blink was a mixture, a mutt. Blink hated the joke and would put on his best longsuffering expression.

"Don't you listen to him," said Danny to the dragon when they were alone in the woods. "I bet you're a pure bred dragon and that's what matters. You're probably a… Three-Toed Purple, or a… Violet Arrowtail." Danny was enjoying this game. "Or wait," he said, "maybe you're a Lilac Lovely?"

With a deft claw, Blink flicked sand at Danny's head. Danny ducked, still laughing.

"No, I know what you are," he said, getting to his feet, ready to run. "You're a Mauve Elvis Impersonator!" And he was off, with an angry dragon in hot pursuit.

Danny had not gone twenty paces when he ran into the man. He seemed to have appeared from nowhere. Danny rebounded as if he had hit a brick wall.

"Sorry!" he muttered, as the man steadied him from falling over.

"All right, son. Just look where you're going next time," said a deep, cockney voice. Danny looked up, surprised. Denim jacket, T-shirt with the name of a heavy metal band. The Tattooed Man! For a moment, Danny was petrified. But no, this man had no tattoos and he did have a long ponytail; the other had been bald as a cue ball. It wasn't the same man. Was it? He was still holding Danny by the arms, although Danny was no longer in any danger of falling.

"I'm all right now, thanks, Mister," said Danny loudly, for the benefit of a family just passing on bikes. The man looked round, momentarily distracted, and Danny took the opportunity to squirm out of his grip and run. Blink was close at his heels. They headed straight back to the camp, where Danny made an excuse about his tent being full of ants so he could sleep on the floor of the cabin.

In the middle of the night he woke up in a panic: the man was holding him by the arms and he had a tattoo on the inside of his wrist. It showed some sort of creature, curled round an old-fashioned goblet. Danny thought it might be a dragon…

Danny came to and realised he had been dreaming. There was no one holding him. He lay still and waited for his breathing to return to normal. He tried to remember if the man had had a tattoo on his wrist but he couldn't. He was probably just mixing him up with the Tattooed Man. Danny got up and crossed to the window. Nothing stirred outside. The campsite was calm under the moonlight, but he wished he had not sent the Professor away. He got Vale's card out of his pocket and turned it over in his hands. There was no computer here or he could have sent a coded message. He wondered if this was enough of an emergency to use the mobile number and decided to sleep on it. He lay back down with Blink, but it was a long time before he fell asleep again.

In the morning, things looked brighter, as things usually do. Danny decided not to bother the Professor, just because he had seen a man who looked a bit like another man. He was being stupid. All the same, when Trevor went windsurfing, Danny stayed on the shore with Blink. That evening, they didn't stray far into the woods and they went home early, before it got dark.

"What's up with you?" asked his dad.

"Just enjoying some quality time with my family!" Danny replied.

"Yeah, right!" said Trevor. "I can tell when you're up to something!"

The next day, Danny roved a little further, prompted by Blink who wanted to go hunting. They saw no strange men in the woods. In the evening they had a barbecue and Danny was sent to the shop to get pudding. Danny bought a chocolate cake and turned to leave the shop. That was when he saw the man at the next till, not the one from the woods or from the park: this was a well-dressed man, with short, blond hair, who smiled at the cashier, showing a lot of white teeth.

Danny froze, staring at the man, who was loading three drinks and three chocolate bars into a bag. This time there could be no doubt. Danny had seen him before, at home, near the river. The dog walker who had no dog. And what was that on the inside of his arm? He didn't look the type for a tattoo…

The man looked up and caught Danny staring. Danny summoned all his acting ability and pretended he was checking his change. Then he nodded, put the change in his pocket and walked out of the shop without looking back.

As soon as he was outside, Danny ran down the path, calling for Blink. The dragon came sprinting, thinking it was a game. Together they pelted towards the cabin. Danny stopped only when he could run no more. His breath was rasping and he had a stitch in his side. He glanced behind but there was no one chasing them.

"Stay close!" Danny panted to the dragon. "Must text Vale!"

Vale's number was in his contacts (under U.R. for Uncle Rupert). Danny quickly composed his message: *Men with tattoos everywhere! Please help!*

"Come on, Blink!" he called, starting to run again. But Blink didn't follow, in fact he was nowhere to be seen. Danny slowed to a walk and then stopped, listening. The woods were still and ominously silent.

"Blink!" he called. "Come on boy! This is no time for hide-and-seek!"

Danny strained his ears and thought he heard a twig snap. Suddenly he had a bad feeling. He took a few steps into the undergrowth. "Blink, I'm not joking, come out!"

Danny stubbed his toe on a root, swore and stopped dead, listening again. All he heard was the rustling of trees, and then, suddenly, a car door slammed, not far away.

Danny's bad feeling got very much worse. Ignoring the tearing branches and uneven ground, he began to run as fast as he could through the woods towards where the sound had come from. Now he could see something blue through the trees.

Bursting into a clearing, Danny saw the blond man standing by the back of a blue transit van. The tattooed man and the ponytailed man were heaving a bundled up tarpaulin into the van. Danny knew what was in it even before the tell-tale arrow-tip of Blink's tail slipped out.

"No!" he screamed.

The three men turned to look at him.

"Get him!" ordered the blond man, calmly. The ponytailed man let go of the dragon and came for Danny.

Danny turned to run, but his leg caught on a branch and he went crashing to the floor. The ponytailed man had him pinned down immediately.

"Get off me!" shouted Danny. He struggled and kicked and shouted some more, but the man just laughed and clamped a beefy hand over his mouth. Danny tried to bite the hand, but it was so big that he couldn't open his jaws wide enough.

Blink was in the van now. The blond man was closing the doors, while the tattooed man, on his orders, came towards Danny.

The ponytailed man let go of Danny's mouth, but only long enough for the tattooed man to slap a piece of gaffer tape over it. Then they pulled his hands round behind him and bound his wrists together with more tape. They worked as a team, without speaking and Danny suddenly knew that they were brothers. How stupid he had been not to think of it before. They were binding his ankles now. All the while Danny struggled and fought, shouting muffled swear words through the gaffer tape gag.

"Shut up and keep still!" yelled the tattooed man, and he cuffed Danny round the ear. Stars exploded in Danny's head. His face went down into the dirt and his eyes and nose filled with grit. Then they pulled him up and shoved a sack over his head, pulling it down to his waist and fixing more tape around it.

"What shall we do with 'im, boss? Bring 'im?" asked one of the brothers. Danny wasn't sure which because they sounded just the same.

"Leave him!" ordered the blond one. "More trouble than he's worth! Anyway what's he going to do – phone the police and report a missing dragon?"

There was rough laughter as the two brothers walked away and then Danny heard the van doors slam and the engine start. He shouted and struggled again, but to no avail. He couldn't get up, not even to his knees. The van moved off and the woods were silent.

Danny closed his eyes against the tears he desperately wanted to shed. Crying would not help Blink. He needed a plan. He needed to get out of the sack. He wriggled and writhed on the ground like a worm, while the air in the sack got hotter and staler, but the tape got no looser. If anything it felt tighter. Danny stopped, feeling light-headed and exhausted. He closed his eyes for a while, he wasn't sure how long. When he opened them again, it seemed darker outside. He had wasted time feeling sorry for himself. He could not afford to do that again.

Danny took as deep a breath as he could manage and rolled himself over to one side then the other, feeling for anything that could help him. He was in luck. To his left he felt a tree root sticking up from the ground. A bit of strategic wriggling and he managed to catch the tape on it and pull it loose. A bit more wriggling and he was out of the sack, gratefully gulping the fresh, cool air. Next he began working on the tape that bound his hands, trying to catch it on the same tree root, but he only succeeded in pulling it tighter, until he could feel his wrists were red raw. What he needed was a blade. Suddenly he remembered his penknife. It was a miracle the kidnappers had not checked his pockets.

Slowly, painfully, Danny managed to work his bound hands around to the front pocket of his jeans, all the time aware of minutes passing and darkness falling. His wrists were very sore now and his head was throbbing, but Danny ignored the pain. Pain he could live with. His fingertips touched the knife in his pocket, gradually working it free. It took several minutes to get that far, even longer to pull out the blade and to work it carefully between his wrists. Gingerly, he began sawing at the tape. It was a slow and clumsy process, but the last thing he needed was to cut himself: he could bleed to death before anyone found him.

It seemed like hours before the tape broke and his hands came apart. Danny immediately sat up and ripped the gaffer tape off his mouth. It stung like hell and he swore loudly. Before even untying his feet, he took out his mobile phone. Maybe he couldn't call the police, but he could certainly call Vale. The Professor answered on the second ring.

"They've taken him!" blurted Danny. "I need your help!"

"Where are you? In the woods?"

"On the lake path."

"I'll be two minutes." Vale rang off.

Danny found he was not at all surprised that Vale was only two minutes away. He had probably been there all week, skulking in bushes. With shaking hands, Danny cut the tape that bound his ankles. As soon as he could stagger up, he found his way back to the path. Vale was already hurrying along it.

"Are you all right?" he asked.

"Bit bruised. I'll live." As Danny said this, his legs gave way. Vale helped him sit down on a log, taking off his own jacket and putting it around Danny's shaking shoulders.

"They were waiting for us," Danny explained, through the embarrassing sobs that had engulfed him. "I tried to fight back but they tied me up…" Briefly, he told the story of the ambush. "I'm sorry I was so careless. I should have listened to you!"

"Let's not worry about that now," said Vale. "We've got a dragon to find."

"You know who these people are, don't you?" asked Danny.

"Yes."

"And you know where they've taken him?"

"Yes."

That was all Danny needed to know. "Right," he said, wiping his nose on his sleeve as he struggled to his feet. "Let's go and get him back!"

8

To the rescue!

They had limited time to come up with a plan.

"If you're coming with me… " Vale began.

"Of course I am!" Danny interrupted.

"… then we'll need to throw your parents off the scent," finished Vale. "We can't have the police after us, thinking it's you that's been kidnapped."

He was right, of course. The police might not take a missing dog seriously, but they would certainly mount a search for a missing boy. Danny had to think faster than he ever had in his life. By the time he reached the cabin he had come up with the best story he could manage in such a hurry.

"Don't think about it, just do it!" Vale had advised. "I'll get the car and wait by the gate."

Unfortunately, there was no one at the cabin. Danny had to double back, but he eventually found Trevor in the pub.

Danny took a deep breath and tried his best to

sound excited. "Dad! You'll never guess who I met!"

"Where've you been?" demanded Trevor. "And where's my pudding?"

Pudding? Danny had forgotten about the pudding. It must be lying out in the woods somewhere.

"And look at the state of you!" Trevor went on. "You're filthy!"

"I fell over in the woods," Danny lied quickly. "I squashed the cake! Sorry!"

"Never mind," said Trevor, who must have had quite a few drinks already. "Mum and Sam have gone for ice creams. They're in the café if you want one."

Danny shook his head and tried again. "Dad, you'll never guess who I met!"

"Who?"

"Jason! Jason Bradley, from school. He's on holiday here, too. They arrived today!"

"My, what a small world it is!" muttered Trevor. "I can't believe that!"

"Well, Jason's dad met that same bloke in town and he booked the holiday with him!"

"Oh, I see," said Trevor.

"Thing is, Dad, they've invited me to sleep over with Jason at their cabin. Then tomorrow they're getting up early and going to the beach for the day. They've asked me to go with them. They'll be back in the evening. Can I go?"

"Well, that's kind of them," said Trevor. "I don't see why not."

"Thanks, Dad."

"What about the dog?" asked Trevor.

"Oh, they've invited him, too. They love dogs. He's already with them." Danny swallowed the lump that rose in his throat at the thought of Blink.

"Great," said Trevor. "Get Jason's dad in here. I'll buy him a drink."

"Can't, Dad," said Danny. "They're making me cocoa back at the cabin. It'll be getting cold. I'd better go. See you tomorrow night."

Danny made to leave, but his dad called him back.

"What number is their cabin, just in case?"

"Forty-seven," lied Danny, smoothly.

He leaned in and gave his dad an awkward hug before running out of the bar. When this is over, he thought, I won't lie to them ever again!

Vale was waiting by the entrance, as promised, in a Volvo estate that must have been at least thirty years old. The bonnet was blue, the passenger door red; the rest of the car was two shades of green and five shades of rust. Danny had seen better-looking cars in scrap yards. Gingerly, he opened the creaking passenger door and sank into the seat, literally: the springs were so old and saggy, he felt like he was sitting on the road. Inside, the car smelled of old leather, stale food and sweat. From the assorted debris, Danny concluded that Vale had been living in it.

"All right?" asked Vale.

Danny nodded wordlessly. He had seldom been so far from all right.

Vale turned the key and the car coughed and spluttered before catching. Then the engine revved and the car hopped forwards like a kangaroo, before stalling again. It took five attempts to get it to start properly but, finally, they swung out of the holiday park and onto the road.

Vale was a terrible driver. He went much too fast, always braking at the last possible moment. The tyres squealed on every corner and Danny's seat rocked as he was pitched back and forth. Any moment he thought he really would be sitting on the tarmac. He held on tightly to the door handle, until it came off in his hand.

For a long time neither of them spoke. Danny was slumped in his seat, thinking, what have I done? He was breaking so many of the rules of common sense. He had lied to his parents and gone off with a stranger to who-knew-where in a car that was barely roadworthy. He had even dragged poor, innocent Jason into his scheme. But what else could he do? He had to get Blink back. Right now that was all that mattered.

Danny broke the silence.

"So where are we going, exactly?"

"The Orkneys."

"You think that's where they've taken him?"

"Sure of it."

"How long will it take?"

"About five hours driving, then the ferry," said Vale. "I hope you've got your sea legs!"

After Vale's driving, Danny thought he'd be lucky to have any legs at all.

"On the plus side," added Vale, "they're not far ahead of us. And there's no ferry until morning. Old Bessie'll catch 'em!" He tapped the steering wheel fondly.

If she doesn't fall apart first, thought Danny.

The old man turned and spoke seriously to him. "Don't be afraid, Daniel, I will take care of you." He looked up at the road just in time to swerve back to his own side, narrowly avoiding an oncoming lorry.

Danny didn't attempt conversation again until they reached the main road. Then he asked, "How do you know where these people have taken Blink?"

"They'll have taken him back to the island where I found him."

"Why, is there treasure there?"

Vale nodded slowly, his eyes full of the memory.

"Tell me about the dragons," Danny asked. "From the beginning."

"Are you sure?" asked Vale. "It's a very long story…"

"I'm not going anywhere for the next five hours!" said Danny.

"I was a young research scientist," Vale began. "I was up near the North Pole studying the aurora borealis. Do you know what they are?"

"The northern lights. Yeah, I've seen them on the telly," Danny replied, impatient for Vale to get on with the story.

"Well, I set up instruments to measure electrical energy and I came across a strange energy field. The readings kept fluctuating in a way I couldn't explain. So I stayed up there alone for a few days, camped out in sub-zero temperatures, while I tried to figure it out. And I became aware of things moving around me. I could see them flitting around out of the corner of my eye, but when I turned to look I could never quite catch sight of them. I thought the snow was playing tricks with my eyes, except every time I saw a flicker, the energy field got stronger, until the readings went off the scale. Then one day, when I was scouting around, I discovered the entrance to an ice cave. It was so well concealed that I hadn't noticed it before, but just near it the readings were at their strongest. The entrance was a tight fit but I could just get through so I ventured inside. That was the day I saw my first dragon."

"No kidding? Was it purple?"

"No, this one was blue, quite small, almost dainty."

Danny thought that only Vale could describe a dragon as dainty. "Why wasn't it camouflaged?" he asked.

"I don't know. Perhaps because it was inside the cave. It just didn't bother wasting the energy."

"What did you do?"

"Ran like hell! As soon as the dragon saw me, it screamed blue murder and chased me right out of the cave. I only just made it through the small entrance before it caught up with me! As it was its claws made quite a gash in my leg. I'm only alive now because it didn't dare breathe fire until we were outside the cave."

"Because the ice would have melted!"

"That's right!"

"So how did you get away?"

"I was lucky enough to fall down a crevasse!"

"Lucky? I don't call that very lucky!"

"But it was, you see, because the dragon left me for dead but in fact I didn't fall far. I landed on a ledge, and after a few hours I managed to climb out. I had a broken wrist, a gashed leg, frostbite and hypothermia, but I made it back to base."

"Did you tell people about the dragon?"

"I tried, but no one believed me. They thought the cold had sent me mad! When I was well enough I went back to the place, but the dragon was gone. Since then I've been tracking them all over the world, wherever there are strange energy patterns."

"Like where?"

"The Bermuda Triangle, high up in the Himalayas… I've seen blue dragons in Iceland, and some red ones living on a volcano on a Pacific Island!"

"And what about the Orkneys?"

Vale nodded. "That's where I found him."

"Tell me." Danny was so enthralled that he'd even stopped noticing Vale's terrible driving.

"I moved to the Orkneys to study the energy fields around the islands. I was sure there were dragons there. One day, I was out on my boat, when suddenly all my instruments went haywire, compass and everything!" Vale began. "I didn't have a clue where I was and there was a storm coming in, so I landed on the nearest island and headed inland, looking for shelter. I found a cave, in the side of a mountain. Part of the tunnel had collapsed. I couldn't get through, but I could see that there was a big cavern in there. It seemed to be…lit up somehow. Then I noticed a side passage. It was narrow but I went along it and I found a little round chamber and in the middle a fire pit full of glowing embers. At first, I thought a human had made it. Then I saw an egg, the size of a rugby ball, nestled in the hot coals."

"What did you do?" asked Danny.

"I got out! Where there's a dragon egg, there's a dragon mother, and I didn't want to be trapped in a cave with her, not after the last time! So I hid out in another side tunnel and waited until she came back. She was the first purple I had ever seen and she was so beautiful! I watched her come and go, bringing wood to stoke the fire. She didn't care about the storm that was raging outside! On her last trip she brought a rabbit to eat. After that she stayed in the cave and I fell asleep in my hiding place. In the morning, the storm was over and she was gone so I ventured out to explore the island. I found another entrance tunnel, higher up the hill. It wasn't as badly blocked as the lower one. I set to work digging my way in, and I saw…"

"What?" breathed Danny.

Vale shook his head, as if the memory was too amazing to put into words.

"It was a huge cavern, shaped like a cone, as if the whole mountain had been hollowed out. There was an opening at the top, like a chimney, so there was daylight coming in, and the cavern was full of treasure, a great pile of it! Gold, silver, precious stones. The whole place seemed to glow…" Vale went silent, remembering the wonders of the cavern.

"What else was there?" prompted Danny.

"A dragon, a great big one, fast asleep on top of the treasure!"

"Was it purple?"

"No, it was green and it was built like a tank, with sharp horns and claws the length of your arm!"

"Were you scared?"

"Not really. I was more amazed than anything. After all the years I had chased dragons, to see two in twenty-four hours was incredible. I could have stayed there and watched all day."

"So what happened?"

A shadow crossed Vale's face. "I did something stupid," he replied.

"What?"

"I leaned in for a better look and I knocked down a loose rock. It went crashing into the treasure pile and the dragon woke up!"

"Did it come after you?"

"It did, but it was too big to fit down the tunnel I was in. Instead it breathed fire at me and I had to run for it. As soon as I got out of the cave, it came flying after me!"

"So how did you get away?"

"Pure luck, once again, my boy! Just as it was chasing me down the mountain, it saw the purple mother come out of her cave. It forgot about me and set off after her, screeching and snarling and breathing fire. She flew off and it chased her. Then they disappeared and I never saw either again!"

"So you had to look after the egg?"

"Well, I felt kind of responsible. If I hadn't woken the green dragon, it would never have gone after her. I was very afraid it had killed her. So I sat for four days and kept stoking the fire as best I could. I even slept in the cave so I could keep an eye on the egg, but I was running out of food. I knew I'd have to leave, and I didn't know if I'd ever find my way back there."

"So what happened?"

"The egg hatched!"

"And that was Blink!"

"That's right! So now I had no food and a baby to look after. I knew I had to take him home with me, or he would die."

"But how did you know how to look after him?"

"I didn't. I just had to guess! I kept him warm by the fire. I fed him meat, eggs and milk, anything I could find really. And I kept him hidden. Then, by accident, my neighbour saw him and, lo and behold, he was a puppy!" Vale cackled at the memory, but Danny could imagine what a relief it must have been for him. "The rest you know," he finished.

Danny thought for a while about Vale's story.

"So Blink really has got treasure?" he mused.

"Oh, yes. To these people, he's as good as a treasure map. You see, dragons have a powerful homing instinct. These men think, if they take Blink back to the islands, he'll return to the cave and lead them to the treasure."

"But how will they follow him?"

"With some kind of tracking device, I imagine."

Danny thought for a few moments.

"And if Blink does lead them to the treasure," he asked in a small voice, "what will they do with him then?"

Vale did not answer but a shadow crossed his face and the car engine raced harder.

9

All at Sea

They drove until two in the morning, before stopping at a truck stop for petrol.

"And coffee!" said Vale. "Before I fall asleep!" He caught sight of Danny's anxious expression. "Don't worry, we've got time. We'll easily make the morning ferry."

Before they went into the café, Vale pulled down his baseball cap and tucked his plait down inside his jacket. "Best to keep a low profile," he explained. "Perhaps you should call me Grandad?"

"Not Uncle Rupert?" asked Danny, pulling up the hood of his sweatshirt.

Vale shook his head. "I'm not in an Uncle Rupert mood tonight," he replied.

"Whatever," said Danny. "As long as I don't have to be Davina!"

Danny thought he was far too worried to eat anything but as soon as he stepped into the steamy café with its welcoming smell of grease and tea, he was starving. 'All Day Breakfast' read a sign, and it wasn't kidding. They both tucked in to bacon, eggs, sausage, beans and toast. Danny drank sweet tea, and Vale downed three mugs of coffee.

The café was almost empty, and the few truckers eating there took little notice of an old man and a boy.

"I like these places," said Vale quietly to Danny. "You can be anonymous!"

"Yeah, I like them too: I've been to loads with my dad."

"Indeed, it was in just such a place that I met your father!" agreed Vale.

"When you gave him Blink?"

"That's right. We'd met a few times and we got talking about families. He told me he was very worried about his son. How he had a lying habit – he was a loner, no real friends, being bullied..."

Danny squirmed in his seat to think of his dad talking to a stranger about him.

"So I seized my chance," Vale continued. "I asked if he'd considered a pet, and I fed him a sob story about this puppy I had to get rid of."

"He told me," said Danny. "It sounded like a lie!"

"Your father fell for it!" said Vale.

"He never learns!" grinned Danny. "But how did you know I'd take care of him?"

"I didn't! I took a chance! That's why I've been keeping an eye on you ever since! And I have to say, you've done a great job!"

"Until tonight," said Danny. He pushed his plate away, unable to eat any more.

When they got back in the car they travelled on without speaking. Vale put on an all-night radio station. Danny was sunk down in his seat and his misery. He blamed himself for leading Blink into a trap, for not fighting off the kidnappers. He wished he could put the clock back and do things differently. Tears pricked the back of his eyes and he closed them tightly. It was not many minutes before he was asleep.

When Danny woke he heard seagulls. The car was stationary and Vale was gone. A cold grey light through the window told him it was dawn.

Danny stretched his aching limbs and struggled out of the car: he was dying for a pee. They were at the docks. Danny headed for the toilets and met Vale coming out.

"Be quick! We're about to board the ferry," said Vale.

They drove onto the ferry and, before going up to the passenger lounge, they took a good look around the car decks for a blue transit van. There was none on board.

"So where are they then?" asked Danny.

"We can't have overtaken them," Vale mused. "So either they've changed vehicles or caught a different ferry: there are other ferry companies and other routes."

"Great! So we've lost them!" said Danny.

"No we haven't. We know where they're going."

"But they could be ahead of us?"

"It's possible."

"By how much?"

"I don't know. Not more than an hour or so."

"An hour? How can you be so calm?" yelled Danny. In an hour they could easily find the treasure and kill Blink.

"Don't shout. You're drawing attention to us," said Vale. Catching sight of Danny's expression, he added, "They don't know the islands as I do. We can make up the time, I'm sure."

He turned away from Danny and made a call on his mobile phone. Danny overheard him ask someone to 'check the weather instruments'.

"My assistant," he explained, as soon as he had put the phone down. Then he stretched out on a bench, put his cap over his face and immediately began to snore.

The ferry journey took two hours, and Vale slept for all of it, while Danny stared out at the horizon without seeing it. His all day breakfast churned uncomfortably in his stomach until he was not sure he would be able to keep it all day.

Back in the car, they did not speak at all on the half hour journey to the north side of the island.

Vale's house, if you could call it a house, was down a dirt track, miles from anywhere. It was little bigger than a mobile home: a single story cottage with white walls, a low thatched roof and two tiny windows. In the yard outside, two chickens were pecking.

As they approached, the door opened and a girl of about Danny's age emerged. She was wearing jeans and a red checked shirt several sizes too big for her. Her auburn hair was pulled back from a freckled face and she wore a huge grin, which faded to puzzlement as she saw Danny.

"Who's she?" asked Danny.

"That's my assistant, Beth," Vale explained, jumping out of the car to greet her.

"But she's just a kid!" muttered Danny, as he got out of the car.

"Welcome home, Professor," Beth was saying in a melodic, Scottish lilt. "You didn't tell me you'd be bringing anybody!" She cast a curious glance at Danny.

"Now, Beth, you know I don't say more than I need to on the phone."

"I know," she said, rolling her eyes slightly. "You never know who might be listening!"

"This is Daniel," Vale told her.

"The dragon boy?" she asked, looking at him with renewed interest. "Then where's…?"

A glance into the car told her the answer and her face fell. "Oh no!"

Vale nodded, "He's been taken."

"Them?" she asked.

Vale nodded again.

"No wonder you asked me to check the instruments," she said.

"Has there been anything?" asked Vale, hurrying towards the house.

"Aye!" she answered, following, "They lit up about an hour ago. I knew something was the matter." And they disappeared into the house, leaving Danny standing forgotten in the muddy yard with the chickens.

When no one came out to get him, Danny shrugged and followed them into the house. Inside, it was dark and cluttered. A battered sofa by the fireplace told him he had stepped into the main living room; an ancient fridge and cooker told him this must also be the kitchen. The table, and every other surface, was covered with piles of books and papers. At the far end of the room was a doorway and through it he could hear Vale talking rapidly to Beth. Danny poked his head round the door and saw a bed pushed into one corner. The rest of the space was taken up with a variety of scientific instruments. Vale and Beth were huddled around a computer screen, which was displaying a lot of figures.

"They're here all right!" said Vale. "There has been dragon activity around the islands all morning."

"So where are they?"

He and Vale leant over a map. "We're here," said Vale, pointing to the northern tip of the big island. "And the readings are coming from here." It was a group of tiny islands off to the west, that wasn't even marked with a name. "That's near where I found him!"

"So how do we get there?" asked Danny. He was pretty sure there wouldn't be a ferry.

"We'll take *Little Susie*," said Vale, leaving Danny none the wiser. The Professor turned to Beth. "Is there any food in the house?"

She nodded. "My mother sent bread, butter and milk."

"Your mother's a saint," pronounced Vale.

"Can I come with you?" Beth asked. "You said I could, the next time."

Vale did not answer immediately.

"What kind of sailor are you, Daniel?" he asked instead.

Danny merely shook his head. He was no kind of sailor at all.

Vale turned back to Beth. "You can crew for me, if your parents will allow it."

"Ach, you know they will! I'll go and ask them!" She left the house at a run.

Vale turned away and busied himself gathering the instruments he would need.

"Can I help?" asked Danny, after he had been ignored for several minutes.

"Yes," said Vale. "Make sandwiches!"

Danny flushed with indignation but thought better of saying anything. He retired to the kitchen and found the makings of jam sandwiches.

"Make as many as you can," instructed Vale, from the bedroom, so Danny used the whole loaf of bread.

"And a flask of tea," called Vale.

"Yes, sir!" muttered Danny.

He turned on the ancient-looking tap. It coughed and spluttered, but provided enough water to fill the kettle. He poked through the untidy cupboards and found a large, stale-smelling thermos flask. He washed it out as best he could before filling it with strong, sweetened tea. He was packing the food into a rucksack when Beth returned. She had put on a sweater and a waterproof coat and brought apples and chocolate biscuits to add to the feast.

"Mum's fine about me going. Here!" She handed Danny a waterproof. "It belonged to my brother, Toby, but he's grown out of it now."

Danny reluctantly accepted the coat. He didn't like Beth: she was far too cocky. And why had Vale never mentioned her before?

"Put this on too," said Vale, throwing him a luminous orange life-jacket. "Beth will show you how."

"I don't need one. I can swim!" he protested.

"No life-jacket, no trip," said Vale, firmly, and Danny had to suffer the indignity of letting Beth strap him into the thing.

"He makes me wear one, too," she said, trying to be encouraging. Danny only scowled at her.

Then they were walking down to the boat, each of them loaded with supplies and equipment.

"Your mum must really trust the Professor," Danny said to Beth. He couldn't imagine his own mum being so cool about a sailing trip. Fortunately, she thought he was at the seaside with Jason.

"My parents are good friends with the Professor," she explained. "My dad was a scientist too, before they dropped out and came to live here on the island. My mum was a doctor. They're hippies," she added, with a roll of the eyes. "We used to live in Edinburgh 'til we came here. My parents said we were going to live 'the good life'."

"What's that when it's at home?" asked Danny.

"Well, mainly it means having no money and being knee-deep in pig poo!"

Danny laughed in spite of his resolution not to like her.

"Anyway, the Professor started tutoring me, because I'm…" She broke off, embarrassed.

"Extremely gifted," Vale finished for her. "Beth is a maths genius! Pretty good at science, too."

"Professor!" Beth complained, blushing. Then she caught sight of Danny's expression. "And there's no need to look at me like that, just because I'm a girl!"

"I wasn't!" protested Danny. She's impossible, he thought.

"I'm going to a boarding school on the mainland in September," she continued. "The Professor helped me get a scholarship. I can't wait to get off the island!"

They soon reached a small, natural harbour at the foot of the cliffs where they loaded the gear into a dinghy and rowed out to Vale's sailing boat. *Little Susie* certainly lived up to her name. Danny wasn't sure what he had been expecting but certainly something less flimsy. She was built of wooden planks, about five metres in length. There was a tiny cabin at the front, but the rest of the boat was completely open. The sea looked suddenly very big.

Danny clambered aboard with the others. He had never felt so clumsy and awkward; the boat pitched with his every movement. Vale and Beth deftly set about making the boat ready. Wherever Danny sat, he seemed to be in their way. He was relieved when Vale stationed him in the cabin with the electrical equipment.

"Your job will be to keep an eye on those readings, see if they change. We'll head for this island where all the activity is," he said, stabbing a stubby finger at the map. "When we get near enough, we can follow this," he added, showing Danny a small, handheld monitor a bit like a sat nav. "You'll need to turn it on once every five minutes, to see if we're in range yet."

"In range of what?"

"Of your dragon! This machine can track him!"

Hope and wonder washed over Danny.

"But how is that possible?"

"Because I injected a micro-chip into him before I gave him to you, and this machine can track it. One of my own inventions!" said Vale, looking very smug.

"That's how you always found us! So how close do we have to be?"

"Within two miles."

Danny was excited. The little tracker was like a piece of real spy equipment. When he turned it on, it showed an outline map of the islands around them.

"If he's near, you'll see a little red flashing dot," explained Vale. "Now don't waste the battery!"

Danny hastily turned the tracker off again. Then Vale pulled up the anchor and they set sail. For a while Danny had no time to think of Blink.

Vale sat in the stern of the boat, holding the tiller to steer. Suddenly he shouted, "Ready about! Lee-oh!"

Then lots of things happened at once. Vale shoved the tiller across and the boat swung round; Beth moved from one side to the other, neatly ducking under the sail as it swung the opposite way across the boat, and Danny fell off his seat. Beth erupted into fits of giggles, though she continued to expertly manage the two ropes she was holding.

I hate her, thought Danny as he picked himself up off the floor of the boat. He had just got settled back onto his bench in the cabin when Vale shouted again, "Ready about! Lee-oh!"

This time Danny hung on and did not fall, but as the boat went round, he felt his stomach lurch in the opposite direction. It continued to do that every time they went about, which they did often. Danny began to feel distinctly queasy. To take his mind off it, he tried peering out through the tiny window at the front of the cabin, then wished he hadn't. There were only two other boats in the harbour and they were about to hit one of them. Danny shouted a warning but, as he did so, they went about again, missing the other boat by less than a metre. Beth laughed again at him.

"It's not like a car," she said. "Boats turn instantly. We were nowhere near hitting it. The Professor's a good sailor!"

Danny wasn't convinced. If Vale's sailing was as good as his driving, they were all in trouble. He hunkered down in the cabin, scowling. *I hate her, I hate her, I hate her,* he thought, and he kept quiet as they narrowly missed the other moored boat. Then they were out into open water where there were no other boats to hit. Instead, there were waves that made the small vessel pitch up and down and Danny's stomach with it. He clung to the side of the cabin, certain they would capsize at any moment.

"Ready about! Lee-Oh!"

Danny almost fell off again. He had not expected to keep changing direction now they were out of the harbour.

"It's called tacking," Beth explained, though Danny had not asked. "We have to go back and forth because we're sailing into the wind."

"Won't that take longer?" Danny asked.

"A bit, but at least the sea's calm. That should help us make better time."

Calm? Thought Danny. This is calm? He imagined the blond man with his neat clothes and very white teeth. He couldn't imagine he was travelling in a flimsy little sailing boat, shouting orders while his two thugs pulled on ropes. No, Danny would have bet anything that the kidnappers had a motorboat. He hunkered down and tried to hold on to the contents of his stomach.

"Are you checking those readings, boy?" asked Vale sternly, and Danny remembered he had a job to do. He peered at the screen, trying to steady it against the pitching of the boat.

"No change," he reported.

"Try the tracker."

Danny fiddled with it then shook his head. He was finding it hard to speak even a word.

"If you're going to puke," said Beth with a grin, "don't puke into the wind!"

A few minutes later this advice proved extremely useful.

10

The Island

Danny's torture went on for what seemed like hours. In fact, it was only an hour and a half, during which Vale and Beth drank tea, ate biscuits, talked and joked. All Danny could do was sit in the bottom of the cabin, feeling wretched. Eventually, he stopped throwing up but only because there was nothing left inside him. He still felt sick as a dog. He could barely even concentrate on the instruments and, once, Beth had to come and read them for him.

"I can do it!" he snapped at her, determined to concentrate. After a few more minutes, however, the monitor went crazy and showed nothing but grey fuzz. Danny tapped it but that did no good. Then Vale called out that his compass had gone awry, too.

"This is just what happened the day I found him!" he said. Danny caught his meaning: it must be dragon energy that was interfering with the equipment. "Turn the tracker on!" Vale instructed. "It's the only thing that will still work."

Danny turned the tracker on and this time a little red dot flashed near the top of the screen.

"He's here!" shouted Danny. "That way! We need to go that way!"

His hopes soared and his sickness was forgotten as they wove between islands, drawing ever closer to the flashing dot on the monitor. The islands here were tiny and close together. It was hard to see which one they were heading for until, rounding a headland, they spotted a smart motorboat moored just off shore.

"This is it!" cried Vale. He quickly brought *Little Susie* about and they ducked back behind the headland before they could be seen. There was a small sandy beach in the bay: Vale lifted the centre plate and ran the boat straight up it. Beth was ready and jumped out onto the beach to secure the anchor. Danny was straight out after her, wanting only to be on dry land. The relief! His legs felt wobbly as if the ground was moving beneath him.

They paused for a few minutes while Vale made him drink some of the hot tea. Danny was glad of it, but he refused the offer of a sandwich. Then they stashed the bag of food between some rocks and set off on foot.

The island was mainly rock. The bay where they had landed was surrounded by tall cliffs and there was no way up. They had to clamber over the headland to the next bay, where the motorboat was moored. Vale made them go cautiously, hiding amongst the rocks while they spied on the beach. It was a broad expanse of sand with a stream running down its middle to the sea. A rubber dinghy had been pulled up onto the sand but there was no sign of Blink or the kidnappers.

"So where are they?" Danny asked.

"Heading inland, I expect, looking for the cave." Vale pointed to a rocky hill that rose up in the centre of the island. "It's in there."

"You lead the way, then!" said Danny.

"We'll have to be careful, they may have left a guard," Vale cautioned them.

He set off around the edge of the beach, making them skulk close to the rocks. When they reached the stream, they followed its path inland, through scrubby undergrowth, keeping their heads down, glad of the cover. In places the stream formed short waterfalls, and they had to climb steep, slimy rocks. Otherwise it was a steady uphill scramble. Soon they could see the island's central peak.

Vale, in the lead, suddenly motioned to the two children to get down. They crept towards a little crest in the rocks and saw what he had seen – the cave mouth and a man standing guard in front of it. It was the ponytailed man. He was smoking a cigarette and casually holding a rifle. The sight of it made Danny's stomach clench.

They backtracked a little and considered their options.

"The others must be inside, trying to clear a way through," whispered Vale. "I say we head for the higher opening – chances are they don't even know it's there!"

Danny and Beth nodded their approval of the plan, and the three headed around the hillside, keeping to the undergrowth. Once they were out of sight of the man, they began to climb. There was no cover here so they had to move fast.

"If they've gone in that way, it's good news for us," puffed Vale as they climbed. "They'll waste a lot of time working to clear a way through the rock falls. We could beat them to it yet."

This thought cheered them all and their pace quickened. Vale led them expertly to a barely visible crack in the side of the hill. You would have missed it if you didn't know what to look for.

"It's pretty narrow," warned Vale, "but it gets easier further in." He patted his fat stomach and said, "If I can get through, you'll have no problem! But we must be very quiet. Those men are coming in through the lower tunnel and they'll hear any noise we make."

Torch in hand, Vale led the way into the mountainside. Beth followed, while Danny brought up the rear. Progress was slow and they soon lost the daylight. The torch did little to light the tunnel. Danny felt his way, grazing his knuckles on the rough walls. They rounded a bend and the passage widened, as Vale had promised. Danny was excited to see a chink of golden light up ahead, coming through a gap above a pile of rocks. Motioning the two children to stay still, Vale approached the gap.

"We'll have to make the hole bigger," he whispered, coming back to them. "There's been a new fall since I was here."

They formed a human chain, Vale, very gently, picking rocks off the pile and passing them back to Beth, who passed them to Danny, who carefully placed them on the ground. All the while they were careful not to make any noise. Danny was terrified the Professor would knock a rock down, as he had done before, and alert the kidnappers to their presence. It seemed an age before, finally, Vale had made a hole large enough to poke his head through. He turned, a huge grin on his face, and beckoned to Beth to take a peek. Danny heard her let out an involuntary gasp as she saw the cavern. She immediately drew back, clapping her hand over her mouth. Her eyes were shining. She moved aside to let Danny wriggle forwards and he saw immediately why she had gasped.

The centre of the hill was hollow, just as Vale had described. Weak daylight came from an opening in the ceiling, reflecting a golden glow from the most enormous pile of treasure Danny could ever have imagined. It must have been ten metres high: gold platters and goblets, coins, crowns, strings of precious stones, all heaped together into one glorious mound. Perched right on top, like the king of the world, was Blink.

Blink was unhurt as far as Danny could see, though he was wearing some sort of heavy collar with a box on the side. Presumably that was the treasure-seekers' tracking device. It was nothing like as neat as Vale's micro-chip, but it must have done the job: he had led them to the treasure. The little dragon sat proudly atop his pile of wealth, unaware of the danger he was in. Danny might have cried out but Vale grabbed his arm, pointing at a place lower down in the cavern where stones were beginning to move. Seconds later, a hand emerged from the tunnel that had been blocked, pushing a pile of rocks in front of it that tumbled onto the floor of the cavern. Blink hissed a warning. The man, undeterred, continued to push until he could get his head, and finally his body, through the gap he had made. The blond man stood up and brushed dust off his clothes, letting out a long whistle of admiration as he surveyed the treasure.

A second head appeared, this one completely bald. The tattooed man was bigger and it took him a few moments to struggle out of the tunnel mouth and get to his feet. His eyes too, roamed over the pile of treasure. Instead of a whistle, he let out a string of swear words. Then the two men started laughing, picking up treasures from the pile and showing them to each other. The blond man tried on a crown of gold with what looked like a giant ruby in the centre.

"We're set up for life!" he said, clapping the other on the back. "Now I know how Aladdin felt!"

The bald man laughed, draping a heavy gold chain around his neck. The blond one picked up a shiny silver tray and they used it to show each other their reflections, both of them laughing and posing.

All the while, Blink grew more agitated on top of his pile of wealth. He had stood up and was weaving from side to side; growling now, smoke puffing from his nose.

The men looked up at him and the blond one spoke. "Get rid of that, will you? I don't think we need it anymore!"

They laughed cruelly, and the tattooed man raised a rifle, pointing it straight at Blink.

"No!" shouted Danny, and then everything happened in slow motion.

The dragon turned at the sound of Danny's voice. The tattooed man turned too, pulling the trigger as he did so. Vale pushed Danny's head down and the bullet ricocheted off the cavern wall just above him.

Danny shook Vale off and peered out again. The tattooed man was already taking aim at the dragon.

"Fly!" shouted Danny and Blink took off immediately, flying in circles round the cave, roaring and sending jets of fire down on the two men. They retreated behind some rocks. The blond man was shouting at the tattooed man to get on with it, but every time he took aim, Blink sent another fiery deluge down on him. A second bullet pinged off the cave wall and the tattooed man swore.

Blink tried to fly to Danny but Danny shooed him away.

"Not here!" he said. "It's too small! Get out the way you came in!"

Blink swooped away just in time, as the third bullet dislodged a piece of stone which grazed Danny's forehead as it fell.

Vale had retreated into the passageway with Beth. He tried to drag Danny back too, but Danny would not leave until Blink was safely out. The dragon circled as the man shot wildly, missing every time. Why doesn't he get out? Danny wondered. Then Blink rose higher, heading for the chimney-like passage at the top, making ever-smaller circles. Danny could see his problem now: the chimney was narrow. To enter it he would need to stop circling and when he did he would make an easy target for the gunman.

Danny ducked back into the passageway and picked up a few good-sized stones. Back at the cave entrance he shouted, "Now!" and began hurling rocks at the tattooed man. His aim wasn't great but that didn't matter. The man lowered his gun and put an arm up to protect himself, while the dragon made it up the narrow chimney and disappeared.

"Yes!" cheered Danny.

The gunman fired two more useless rounds after the retreating dragon. Pieces of rock fell onto the pile of treasure, making loud clanging sounds.

"Leave it!" instructed the blond man. He was already loading treasure into sacks.

"Let's go," mouthed Vale and Danny was about to obey when a screech and a crash drew his attention back to the cavern. He was just in time to see Blink re-emerge from the chimney, roaring and breathing fire. He had not made it out of the tunnel at all, and the reason came hard at his heels and roaring twice as loudly: a huge, green dragon built like a tank.

11

Pursuit

The green dragon was twice Blink's size and as ugly as it was aggressive. Its body was muscular, its wings stubby but powerful. On its head were two vicious horns. This was surely the dragon that Vale had described. Instead of having scales like Blink, it appeared to be armour-plated.

The green dragon let out a screech of rage that made Danny's teeth rattle in his head. It was chasing Blink ruthlessly, ready to duel to the death for its treasure. It struck out with enormous claws and Danny saw a gash appear in Blink's side. Drops of thick, purple blood fell into the treasure pile. Blink tried to outfly the green dragon, but there was nowhere to go in the circular cavern.

The tattooed man, in a panic, had raised his rifle again. Danny heard a bullet hit the wall of the cave, then the green dragon swooped and the man threw down his weapon and hit the floor, hands over his head. The green dragon was more concerned about Blink than the humans, though. Rising again, it caught up with him, this time slamming him into the cavern wall. Blink lost height, then recovered, coming back bravely at his attacker. His claws made a gash in its shoulder, then he washed it with fire. The green dragon retaliated with its own huge jet of flame and Danny had to duck behind his pile of stones. The heat was intense but, when the smoke cleared, neither dragon looked harmed. Then the green dragon swiped viciously at Blink, slamming him into the cavern wall again. This time Blink crumpled and dropped like a stone, disappearing behind the pile of treasure.

"No!" wailed Danny, but his shout was drowned out by the screeching of the green dragon. It had turned its attention to the two men below. The gunman was back on his feet and they were both stuffing treasure into sacks as quickly as they could. The dragon dived, roaring in frustration, and sent a jet of flame their way. The blond man screamed in pain. His shirt had caught fire. The tattooed man used an empty sack to smother the flames. The green dragon was in a towering rage now. It breathed fire in every direction as it circled its cavern, raking the walls with its claws and sending chunks of rock raining down on the men. One of them hit the tattooed man on the head and he clutched at the wound, which was pouring with blood. He scrabbled for the way out, his gun forgotten, but the blond man, despite his burns, was still trying to stuff treasure into his sack.

"The fool," Danny heard Vale say beside him.

The green dragon was now alternately dive-bombing the men and hurling itself at the cavern walls. There were scorch marks everywhere and Danny felt a tremor every time the dragon slammed into the rock. More and more stones were falling, as cracks began to appear in the walls.

"We've got to get out," said Vale. "This place could collapse at any moment!"

"I can't leave him!" Danny protested.

"You can't do anything for him!" Vale replied.

Danny looked desperately for a way into the cavern but the opening was too small for him to get through. All he could do was watch.

The blond man had pushed his way into the tunnel behind the other but he seemed to be stuck, his legs sticking awkwardly out of the hole. The green dragon dived at him, gashing his leg with its claws. Danny heard the man's muffled cry of pain, then his injured leg finally disappeared into the tunnel. The dragon continued to pound the cave walls, though it already looked quite battered itself. A trickle of dust rained down on Danny, followed by a few small rocks. Danny looked up and saw that the roof of the tunnel was beginning to crack.

"Come on! You're no good to him dead!" hissed Vale, tugging at his sleeve, but Danny remained, obstinately staring at the place where his dragon had fallen.

"Blink!" he shouted.

Blink did not reappear, but the green dragon heard his cry, and flew straight at the mouth of their tunnel.

"Run!" yelled Vale, and this time Danny obeyed, pounding down the corridor after the others. He staggered as the dragon hit the entrance, causing the whole tunnel to shake. A good many more stones rained on him, but fortunately the opening was not big enough to let even the dragon's head through. In frustration it let out a jet of flame, which shot down the tunnel behind them. Danny ran as he had never run before, the fire rapidly catching up with him. Beth was already out, but Vale slowed as he approached the narrow entrance. Danny, head down, crashed into his back, pushing him through like a cork out of a bottle. Together they tumbled out onto the grass, as the jet of flame spurted above their heads.

Danny lay still, panting. He had fallen on Vale, who lay motionless beneath him. Then Beth was running towards him shouting, "Danny! You're on fire!"

She dragged Danny onto the ground, rolling him over until his burning sleeve was out. Then she sat down beside him, while they both tried to catch their breath. Danny knew his shoulder was burnt but, remarkably, he felt no pain. Beth, meanwhile, was kneeling beside the Professor. He lay motionless, face down, where he had fallen.

"Is he all right?" asked Danny, struggling over to her.

"He's out cold. Must have hit his head! Help me roll him over!"

Between them, they managed to roll the stout form of the Professor onto his back. Danny saw immediately that there was a rock sticking up out of the ground: Vale must have hit his head on it as he fell. Sure enough there was a nasty cut on his forehead, an egg-sized bruise already forming around it.

Beth reached into her pack for a bottle of water and splashed it on the Professor's face. Then she slapped him gently on the cheeks.

"Come on, Professor, you need to wake up!" she called, but the Professor did not stir. "Ach, that always works in the movies!" she complained. While she continued trying to wake the Professor, Danny crept round the hill to where he could look down on the cave mouth. Hiding himself among the rocks, he peered over.

He could see the guard looking around wildly at the noise from inside the cave, waving his rifle here and there, as if unsure where the danger was coming from. Danny ducked back behind his rock before the man saw him. He glanced at the top of the hill where Blink must surely appear.

"Come on boy," he said under his breath, willing the dragon to get out of the cave. The hillside continued to shake beneath them and they could hear the roars and screams of the green dragon inside.

Danny sneaked another look at the guard, just in time to see the blond man burst out of the tunnel mouth. He was limping badly, covered in dust but he was carrying two sacks of treasure. The guard ran to support him, looking back at the tunnel mouth for the third man. Danny saw the blond man shake his head. The ponytailed man set off towards the entrance, and Danny knew he was going to try to save his brother. But the blond man stopped him, still shaking his head. Even from that distance, Danny heard the ponytailed man's muffled shout of 'No!' and knew that the tattooed man was dead. The two thieves began shuffling towards the beach, one supporting the other, each carrying a sack of treasure.

"Danny," called Beth, "he's coming round!"

Danny hurried back to her. Together they helped the Professor sit up.

"Mildred, is that you?" asked Vale.

Beth cast a worried glance at Danny. In other circumstances, they might both have laughed.

"It's me, Professor – Beth!" she said.

"Where's Mildred? Has she come home yet?" asked the Professor.

"I don't know, Professor, but we need to go now. We need to get off this hill!"

With her help and Danny's, Vale managed to get to his feet. He was very woozy and had to put an arm around each of them for support. Pain seared through Danny's shoulder as the Professor put his weight on it.

"If we can just make it to the bushes…" said Beth.

Danny hesitated, turning to look at the hilltop, willing the familiar purple shape to emerge.

"You can't help him," said Beth gently, reading Danny's mind. "But you can help the Professor."

Reluctantly, Danny obeyed. They began to stagger down the hill, but had gone only a few paces when the ground shook beneath them and they all stumbled. Danny looked round to see the green dragon bursting from the top of the hill. It looked quite the worse for wear, covered in dust, with several gashes that oozed dark green, tar-like blood. One of its wings was bent awkwardly, and it lumbered down the hillside on foot, heading straight towards Danny and the others.

There was nothing they could do, nowhere to hide. They stood frozen, as the dragon bore down on them, the ground shaking with its every step. Danny was more afraid than he had ever been in his life. The dragon was so close now that Danny could see its eyes.

They were an evil red. Closer still and he could smell its sulphur breath. He knew he should turn and run but he was rooted to the spot, the weight of the Professor heavy on his shoulders. The dragon slowed a little and Danny braced himself for the fiery breath that would surely engulf him but, instead of fire, the dragon let out a screech of rage. It had caught sight of the two thieves, heading off into the bushes with their treasure. Danny covered his ears against the shrillness of the sound. The dragon altered its course, thundering on past Danny towards the treasure thieves.

Danny and Beth exchanged glances, amazed to find they were still alive. She too had covered her ears, but to little avail: the dragon's screech had left them both temporarily deaf. As if in a silent movie, they watched the two thieves reach the undergrowth, as the dragon quickly closed the gap. The blond man was moving slowly, his leg badly damaged. The ponytailed man took one look at the approaching dragon and shoved his companion aside, grabbing the second treasure sack and making a run for the beach. The blond man stumbled sideways, righted himself and made a valiant attempt to keep going, but the dragon caught him in its great jaws, tossing him aside like a rag doll before ploughing on into the undergrowth where the ponytailed man had disappeared.

Beth turned her face away in disgust.

"Come on!" shouted Danny. "We must get to the boat before it comes back for us!" Beth nodded and, together, they dragged the Professor down the hillside.

When they reached the undergrowth, they stayed in its shelter, only emerging when they had reached the far end of the beach. As Danny's hearing returned, he was aware of the dragon crashing through the bushes. The Professor seemed better: he was able to walk almost unaided now. Beth set off over the rocks with him, but Danny risked a backward glance. The dragon had just reached the beach. The ponytailed man was almost at the water's edge, dragging the rubber dinghy with the treasure sacks in it. It was heavy and his progress was slow. Danny saw the man look up at the dragon, look out to sea, tug at the dinghy, look back at the dragon again and, finally, make his decision. Abandoning the dinghy and the treasure, he plunged into the sea and began to swim for the motorboat. He was only just in time: the dragon pounced angrily on the dinghy, puncturing one of the air chambers with its claws. Then it hesitated, surveying the swimming figure.

For a moment, Danny thought the man was in with a chance. Maybe the dragon would give up now it had its treasure. Maybe it hated water as much as Blink did. Maybe its wing was too damaged to fly. But no, the man was only ten metres out when the dragon took off, flying low and lopsided, but flying nonetheless.

It plucked the man out of the water with its claws, dragging him back to the shallows, where it landed on him with all its weight. The man thrashed in the water, trying to get his head up, but the dragon was too huge for him to fight. Danny turned away, unable to watch the man drown, and scrambled over the headland, to join the others.

12

Under Attack

They tried to run but they were knee-deep in water: the tide had come up while they were at the cave and *Little Susie* was completely afloat. Beth pulled the boat in by the anchor chain and Danny jumped aboard. With Beth pushing and Danny pulling, they managed to get the Professor up over the side of the boat. Danny helped him into the cabin, where he fell sideways onto the bench seat, unconscious again. Danny put a rug over him and then returned to help Beth. She was fumbling with the anchor, thigh-deep in freezing cold water. Danny did his best to help but their hands could hardly grasp the metal.

"You'll have to crew for me!" said Beth, as they worked.

"Me? I don't know how!" He had been planning to send her off then return to the cave for Blink.

"Then you'll have to learn! I can't sail her on my own!" She gave a huge tug and finally the anchor came loose. "Hold the boat while I get in and get the sail up!"

Danny did as he was told. He was torn in two, but he knew his duty lay with Beth and the Professor. He would just have to come back for Blink. He didn't know how, but he would have to manage it.

He stood, waist deep, trying to hold the boat while Beth expertly raised the sail. It was hard work and Danny was glad when she shouted to him to jump in. His first attempt missed, but on his second he got one leg hooked over the side. He was just about to haul himself into the boat, when a shadow blocked out the sun above him.

"Look out!" shouted Danny, but Beth had already seen it. The green dragon swooped in low over the rocks and headed straight for the boat, hitting the mast with all its weight. The impact drove the boat away from the beach, and Danny lost his grip and fell backwards into the water. Scrambling to his feet, he saw the mast snap like a matchstick and the little sail crumple, engulfing Beth beneath it. Danny began to wade out towards her, but *Little Susie* was still travelling away from the shore. The dragon had already turned and come back. It landed on the side of the boat and its weight capsized the little craft instantly, the hull turning right over until it was upside down with Beth and the Professor inside it.

Danny dived into the icy water and swam as quickly as he could towards the boat. He could hardly breathe for the cold and the water felt as thick as treacle. It seemed an age before he reached *Little Susie*.

The dragon was perched triumphantly on the upturned hull, casting a beady eye down into the water for its victims. There was no sign of Beth or the Professor. Danny swam round behind the dragon, took a deep breath and dived before it saw him. He came up in darkness under the hull, bumping into something soft. It was Beth, still tangled in the sail. Danny tried to free her but he was running out of breath. Just as he thought his lungs would burst he bobbed up into a pocket of air that was trapped under the upturned hull. Danny took a deep, rasping breath and he pulled Beth into the air pocket. She coughed and gasped, finally struggling free of the sail.

"The Professor!" she whispered and Danny made out his bald head, bobbing among the floating debris. He reached out and pulled the Professor towards him. Vale was breathing and just conscious. The three of them clung to the upturned boat, keeping their heads above water while they tried to catch their breath. Above them, they could hear the rasp of the dragon's claws on the hull.

"How do we get out of here?" Beth asked in a whisper, but they did not need to worry about that for long. The dragon had heard their voices: it began pounding angrily on the hull, raking at the planks with its claws, making a noise like fingernails on a blackboard. The children watched helplessly as a crack started to appear. Then the noise stopped and a red eye peered through the crack, followed by a huge sniffing nostril. The dragon let out another of those ear-splitting shrieks and, even through the hull, it was loud enough to make Danny lose his grip on the boat and go under. He felt Beth pull him up. The dragon was in a frenzy now, digging away at the hull, great pointed claws appearing between the flimsy planks.

"Dive!" shouted Danny, pushing the Professor down and dragging him out of the upturned boat. Beth was right behind him. She caught hold of Vale's other side and together they pulled him as far from the wreckage as possible before surfacing. They were in luck: the dragon was so busy hammering the boat to pieces that it failed to notice them. It really was very stupid, thought Danny.

They kicked out for shore: it was only a few metres away, but the tide had turned and the current was strong. Their teeth chattered with cold now, and their muscles worked slowly. It seemed an achingly long time before they were dragging the Professor up onto the beach, where he promptly passed out again. Unable to move him any further, Danny and Beth collapsed in exhaustion beside him, coughing and shivering uncontrollably, but there was no time to rest. The dragon had spotted them. With an angry shriek, it left the wreckage of the boat and flew for the beach. Danny and Beth scrambled to their knees and tried desperately to drag the Professor away, but he was a dead weight.

And now the dragon was landing on the sand, only metres away from them. It approached slowly, on foot, its head weaving dangerously from side to side. Danny recognised the gesture. Blink did the same when he was preparing to attack. For the second time that day, Danny looked the fearsome dragon in the eye and expected to die. He felt around for a stone and his hand closed around a large one: he was not going down without a fight.

"You run!" Danny told Beth. "I'll distract it!"

"I won't leave you!" said Beth, stubbornly. From the corner of his eye, Danny saw her reach for a stone as well.

The dragon advanced slowly, spinning out the moment like a cat torturing a mouse. Danny had a stone in each hand now, waiting for his chance. When the dragon was near enough he shouted, "Now!" and he and Beth both pelted its head with rocks. Danny's second shot hit the beast just above the eye and it shook its head as if stunned, but then screamed in rage and charged at them. Danny put up his hands in a vain attempt to protect himself. At that moment another shadow zoomed in over his head.

This one was not green; it was purple.

13

Duel

Blink, dusty and blood-stained, flew straight at the green dragon. Taking it completely by surprise, he knocked it clean off its feet and backwards into the water. A terrible screeching ensued as the two dragons wrestled in the churning shallows.

Then Blink broke free and took off, flying out to sea. The dust had washed off now, and Danny could see that he was battered and bleeding, yet he flew with lighting speed. The green dragon gave chase, but its damaged wing was clumsy. It flapped just above the surface, while Blink circled and came in at a dive. Once more he hit the larger dragon at full pelt, knocking it back into the water. It was a moment or two before the green dragon got airborne. Meanwhile Blink had circled round to dive-bomb again. The green dragon lashed out with claws and fire, but Blink was too quick for it, flying up and away before it could touch him. Over and over he dive-bombed the green, each time pushing it further out to sea.

To Danny, watching helplessly from the beach, Blink looked like a sparrow attacking a hawk. He was so much smaller and weaker than the green, even in its damaged state. And yet he was faster, more agile, and much, much cleverer. Miraculously, the sparrow was holding its own.

The waterlogged green was tiring now. Every lash of the claws and every spurt of fire was an effort. Finally, it stopped attacking and simply tried to fly back to the beach, but Blink would not give up. He kept flying round to cut off its route, attacking then retreating before the counter-attack could be launched.

Now Danny saw that the bigger dragon was in trouble. Unable to get back to dry land, it floundered just above the water. Its damaged wing trailed uselessly. Its fire sputtered and failed. Dollops of tar-like blood oozed from a gash in its side, plopping heavily into the sea. Under Blink's constant attack, the green dragon was losing height. Its back legs disappeared under the water, its body sinking to join them until only its head broke the surface. As Blink came round for another attack, the green made a valiant effort to rise up. Its head and neck broke the surface and its front leg swiped from below the water to catch Blink unawares. Another deep gash appeared on Blink's shoulder and he screeched with rage as he flew out of range. Dive-bombing once more, Blink landed his full weight on the green head, pushing it under the waves. It resurfaced twice, only to be knocked back again: the third time, it did not come up.

Blink stayed, hovering, above the place where the green dragon had disappeared, but only bubbles broke the surface. Satisfied that his enemy was dead, he skimmed back to the beach, landing lightly beside Danny and licking his face in greeting.

Danny managed to raise his arms and put them around Blink's neck. There the two stayed for some time, too exhausted to move.

Beth, too, lay panting on the sand. It was only when the Professor began to stir that she struggled up to kneel beside him.

"How are you?" she enquired.

"Mildred! There you are! I've been looking all over!" said Vale, and this time both children laughed with relief.

"And how are you?" she asked Danny.

"Cold, tired and my shoulder hurts like hell!" he reported.

"I'm not surprised! You got quite a burn back there in the cave!"

Danny had almost forgotten the cave: it seemed a lifetime ago. "I didn't really feel it until now!" he said, bemused. He cast a glance down at his shoulder, but regretted it instantly as a wave of nausea overtook him.

"That was adrenaline, keeping you going!" said Beth. "And how are you, my heroic purple friend? That was some rescue!" Blink inclined his head and allowed her to scratch behind his ears.

They were a sorry and soggy little crew huddled on the beach. Beth surveyed them all and made a pronouncement.

"What we need," she said, "is a nice cup of tea!"

Danny laughed, before realising she was serious. They still had food and drink in the rucksack. Using his last ounce of strength, he scrambled up the rocks and retrieved the pack. The four of them feasted on the picnic he had packed all those hours ago. Never had squashed sandwiches and lukewarm tea tasted so good! With Blink's enthusiastic help, they ate every last morsel. Afterwards, their energy and spirits much restored, they set about making plans.

"Time to get off this island!" said Beth.

"But how…?" began Danny. *Little Susie* was floating around out there in a million pieces.

"Well, it seems to me there's a perfectly good motorboat that no one's in a hurry to use!"

"Of course!" said Danny. She really was smart, he thought.

"We'd better get moving. We want to be back before dark," said Beth.

Full of food and renewed hope, they managed to

get to their feet and stumble back across the rocks to the main beach.

The rubber dinghy was still on the sand where the ponytailed man had abandoned it but the left air chamber was badly deflated where the dragon's claws had punctured it.

"Do you think it'll get us there?" asked Beth, looking out to where the motorboat was moored.

"I dunno," said Danny, "but I don't fancy swimming!"

Gingerly, the children loaded the Professor into the good side of the dinghy and pulled it into the water. It sagged quite a lot on the damaged side but it stayed afloat.

"We'll have to go quickly and hope it doesn't sink!" said Danny. He and Beth took an oar each and began rowing out to the motorboat. It was hard work. Danny's shoulder throbbed, but he gritted his teeth and kept rowing. Vale sat in the stern, pale and clammy. The treasure sacks still sat in the bow, weighing the dinghy down. Water was beginning to lap over the edge and slosh around the children's feet.

"We won't make it!" said Beth. "We need to ditch the treasure!"

Danny only hesitated for a moment before nodding. He tried to hold the boat steady with his oar while Beth clambered towards the bow. With difficulty she hoisted first one sack then the other over the side and into the water where they sank immediately. The bow lifted a little and Beth came back and began rowing again. It was still slow going and they were up to their ankles in water when Blink, who was flying above, swooped down and took the mooring rope between his teeth. He flew ahead, pulling the boat and, with Danny and Beth still rowing, they reached the motorboat just as the dinghy began to go under.

The Professor needed a lot of help to clamber into the motorboat. He only just made it before the dinghy sank completely. Beth installed him in a comfortable seat, and then poked around the boat for anything useful.

"Those kidnappers were fair-weather sailors!" she remarked, triumphantly holding aloft an emergency blanket, which she wrapped around the Professor. She went on to find warm coats for Danny and herself, a first-aid kit and a bottle of whisky.

The boat was surprisingly roomy: even Blink could fit in. Danny was glad he would not have to fly. The dragon was looking tired and the wound on his shoulder was still bleeding.

"I'll clean that up once we get going," Beth promised him. She was looking over the controls, mystified. "I'm lost on this one," she confessed. "Give me a sailboat any day!"

"Shove over, then," said Danny. "You can navigate."

He was good with engines: his dad had taught him. He had the motor started in no time, pulled up the anchor and they were off. This was far easier than sailing, he thought. Once he had the steering and the gears worked out, he let her go faster. They were soon speeding across the waves and Danny did not feel the least bit seasick.

Beth busied herself with the first-aid kit. She dabbed at the Professor's head with a wipe, but he pushed her away, saying he was fine and calling her Mildred. He would not let her near Blink's wound either. Instead he poured some of the whisky over it, before helping himself to a large swig. He even offered the bottle to the children, for medicinal purposes. Beth took a small sip and pulled a face.

"No thanks, I'm driving!" said Danny, with a grin.

Blink set about licking whisky off his flank with apparent relish.

"Don't get a taste for that!" Danny warned him.

The dragon let out a particularly loud and disgusting burp.

Danny reached down and patted him. "I missed you," he said.

14

Aftermath

Danny woke up in an unfamiliar bedroom. He had no idea how long he had been asleep. Hours? Days? It took him a while to remember he was at Beth's house. Beth had called her parents when they arrived back at the island, and they had picked them all up from the harbour in their Land Rover. Beth's mother, the doctor, had dressed his shoulder, given him painkillers and put him to bed.

Danny felt around with his feet, but there was no curled-up mass at the end of his bed. He was just thinking of getting up when he became aware of voices on the landing. One, a woman's, was unmistakeably Scottish; the other, unmistakeably Vale.

"…but he really should go to hospital," the woman was saying. "That burn is quite serious."

"Well, it's a little delicate," explained Vale. "His parents don't exactly know where he is…"

"Professor!"

"Anyway, I'm sure your doctoring is as good as any hospital! Can I go in?"

"I'm not sure the dog ought to…" Her voice trailed off as Vale pushed open the bedroom door and Blink bustled in. The dragon leapt on Danny, licking him all over his face, while Beth's mother stood by the door with a disapproving expression.

"Steady on, boy – ow!" said Danny, as the dragon stood clumsily on his shoulder.

"Off you get, now!" Vale told him and, remarkably, the dragon obeyed, moving to the foot of the bed where he curled up, happily.

Vale pulled up a chair and sat down. "How's the patient?" he asked.

"I'm OK. How about you?" Vale had a neat white bandage around his head.

"Oh, I've had worse than a bump on the head in my time," he said.

Beth's mum shook her head at this. "Concussion is not to be taken lightly!" she reminded him. "If I had my way you'd still be in bed! How's the shoulder?" she added, to Danny.

"It's OK."

"Liar, I bet it hurts like hell!" she replied, with cheerful indifference. She was just like her daughter, Danny thought.

"Yeah, it does!" he admitted.

"I'll get you another painkiller," she said, making to leave. "Beth's on her way up with a tray. I imagine you're pretty hungry?"

Now that he thought about it, Danny realised he was ravenous.

"What time is it? I told my parents I'd be back!" He sat up in a panic, then wished he hadn't, as pain seared through his shoulder.

"Don't worry!" replied Vale, easing him back onto the pillows. "You've only been asleep for a couple of hours. You can phone them now – I've got a plan!"

Vale outlined his scheme then Danny phoned. He felt oddly choked up when he heard his mum's voice.

"Where are you Danny? We expected you back by now!"

Danny explained that Jason's dad's car had broken down and wouldn't be fixed until morning. He would stay the night in a Bed and Breakfast with Jason's family.

"I'll see you tomorrow," he promised.

"Make sure you're back by lunchtime. We're going home tomorrow!" she reminded him.

Danny promised he would be there before lunch, then pretended his phone was out of charge and rang off. Sinking back into the pillows, he thought, when this is over, I'll never tell another lie!

Beth brought in a tray with two bowls of homemade

soup and half a loaf of crusty bread. She stayed with them while Danny and Vale wolfed the lot, and the three of them went over and over the day's events, the children filling Vale in on the bits he could not remember.

"What an adventure, though!" Beth kept saying, her eyes shining at the recollection.

"I wonder where all that treasure came from?" Danny mused.

"From centuries of shipwrecks, I imagine," Vale replied. "Think how much history is buried in that cave." He looked a little rueful at the thought.

For a few moments they all contemplated the treasure and Danny could not help thinking of the fortune it must be worth. Still, he thought, better to leave it buried. After all, it didn't really belong to anyone any more.

"How stupid was that green dragon?" asked Danny, breaking the silence. "Destroying the cave with its treasure still inside!"

"Aye, then smashing the boat to pieces while it was sitting on it!" added Beth.

They laughed together.

"What it lacked in brains, it made up for in aggression," observed Vale. "A bit like some people I've met!"

"Yeah," agreed Danny, thinking suddenly of Wayne Smith.

"Purple dragons are the smartest, aren't they, Presley?" said Beth, tickling Blink affectionately under the chin.

"Presley?" echoed Danny.

"Aye, that's what I used to call him, when he lived with the Professor," she said. "Surely you've noticed his wee Elvis quiff?"

"Of course I have! Only he doesn't like me to mention it!"

Blink, in confirmation, turned his head away.

"Professor," said Danny suddenly. "Can we ask you something?"

"Fire away!"

"Who's Mildred?" asked Danny, and Beth collapsed into giggles.

"Mildred?" asked Vale. "I've never known a Mildred in my life!"

Danny slept like a log that night. Beth's mum's painkillers were so strong they knocked him out. Early next morning, he said his goodbyes and got into Beth's father's car. He was lending it to them for the journey home, and Beth's brother Toby was going to drive it, since Vale was not yet well enough. Beth gave Danny a scrap of paper as he left. It had her address written on it.

"You will keep in touch, won't you?" she asked, anxiously.

"Probably not. I am a boy, you know!" Danny grinned.

Toby was a much better driver than Vale but he knew nothing of dragons, so they could not discuss their adventure. Danny took another painkiller and slept the journey away.

They stopped once at a service station and Danny woke up enough to take Blink for a walk. Vale came with them, while Toby went to the loo. It was their only chance to talk openly.

"What will you do next?" Danny asked the Professor.

"Same things I always do," Vale replied. "Watch the readings and go wherever the dragons are!"

"Will you still come and see us?" Danny realised he would actually miss the Professor and his eccentric ways.

"Oh, I'll pop up from time to time. Just look out for talking bushes!"

Danny laughed. "Is it safe to phone, now those men are out of the way?" he asked.

"Absolutely not!" replied Vale. "You never know who else is watching or listening. We must all remain vigilant!"

Danny rolled his eyes and the old man caught the expression.

"You can email, occasionally," he relented.

"Thanks, Uncle Rupert!"

"You're welcome, Davina!"

Praise for SARAH MOORE FITZGERALD

THE APPLE TART OF HOPE

'This novel . . . has hidden powers' *Daily Telegraph*

'Young readers will be hooked from the get-go' *People*

'A moving and poignant tale about the redemptive power of friendship' *Louise O'Neill*

A VERY GOOD CHANCE

'A life-affirming read about friendship across a social divide' *Sunday Independent*

'Beautifully handled . . . brave and thoughtful . . . It deserves a wide readership and confirms Moore Fitzgerald's place as one of Ireland's most interesting new children's writers' *Irish Independent*

BACK TO BLACKBRICK

'A tear-jerker with lessons in how to live life to the full' *The Sunday Times*

THE LIST OF REAL THINGS

'Completely beguiling, and funny and tender and
wi

Essex County Council

3013021805859 1

Also by Sarah Moore Fitzgerald

Back to Blackbrick
The Apple Tart of Hope
A Very Good Chance
The List of Real Things

A
STRANGE
KIND of
BRAVE

SARAH MOORE FITZGERALD

Orion

ORION CHILDREN'S BOOKS

First published in Great Britain in 2019 by Hodder and Stoughton

1 3 5 7 9 10 8 6 4 2

Text copyright © Sarah Moore Fitzgerald, 2019

The moral right of the author has been asserted.

*All characters and events in this publication, other than those clearly
in the public domain, are fictitious and any resemblance to
real persons, living or dead, is purely coincidental.*

All rights reserved.
No part of this publication may be reproduced, stored in a
retrieval system, or transmitted, in any form or by any means, without
the prior permission in writing of the publisher, nor be otherwise circulated
in any form of binding or cover other than that in which is it published and
without a similar condition including this condition being
imposed on the subsequent purchaser.

A CIP catalogue record for this book is available from the British Library.

ISBN: 978 1 51010 412 9

Printed and bound in Great Britain by Clays Ltd, Elcograf S.p.A.

The paper and board used in this book are from
well-managed forests and other responsible sources.

Orion Children's Books

An imprint of
Hachette Children's Group
Part of Hodder and Stoughton
Carmelite House
50 Victoria Embankment
London EC4Y 0DZ

An Hachette UK Company
www.hachette.co.uk
www.hachettechildrens.co.uk